CU00692348

CHRISTMAS WITH FRIENDS

(FRIENDS LIKE THESE BOOK 2)

HANNAH ELLIS

This is a work of fiction. Names, characters, places, and incidents either are the products of the author's imagination or are used fictitiously. Any resemblance to actual persons, living or dead, businesses, companies, events, or locales is entirely coincidental.

Text copyright © 2015 Hannah Ellis
All Rights Reserved

Cover design by Aimee Coveney

For Gran and Sal
with love

Chapter 1

My life had changed quite dramatically since I met Brian. Although, it was five o'clock on a Friday afternoon and I was drinking wine alone, so there were still some similarities. Not long ago I'd have been dressed in my pyjamas, lazing on the couch with no plans to move. Now I was wearing a black cocktail dress with sheer black tights and a pair of stilettos.

My hair was freshly cut and coloured, and bounced whenever I moved my head. I wasn't slouched on a grubby old couch either. Nope, I was perched on a barstool in a very ladylike manner in Brian's kitchen. He had such a lovely house. Actually, it was my house now too. Living there still felt a bit odd, like I was on holiday or something. The wine glasses even seemed posh; they made a gentle ting sound when I tapped them with my manicured fingers. Yes, I even had a manicure. I really had changed a lot.

The key clicked in the front door and Brian shouted hello. I kept quiet, but sat up straighter and adjusted my dress to make sure my cleavage was well displayed.

Brian did a double take when he caught sight of me. It was exactly the reaction I'd been waiting for. Obviously this wasn't how he generally found me when he came home from work. Usually I was sprawled on the couch with my pyjamas on and a bottle of wine beside me. Things hadn't changed as much as I'd made out. This was a special occasion.

"Wow." Brian blinked a few times.

I tapped the wine glass and re-crossed my legs in what I hoped was a seductive gesture. It was quite nice the way he was looking at me.

"You look amazing." He came and slipped his arms around my waist and kissed me lightly on the lips. "What's the occasion?"

"Ha ha," I said dryly.

He frowned and a look of panic flashed across his features.

"Brian!" I slapped his chest. "It's the office Christmas party. Did you forget?"

He shook his head. "I thought I'd forgotten your birthday or an anniversary or something."

"So you didn't forget the party?"

"I didn't *forget*. We agreed we weren't going."

My eyes widened. "No we didn't. I told you I wanted to go."

"*I* don't want to go. It's my work party. Surely, I decide."

"No! Of course you don't decide." I growled. He'd drive me mad one day. "I can't even be bothered to discuss this with you. Just get changed. We're going."

He laughed. "No, we're not."

"I'm all dressed up." I'd gone a little high-pitched. "I've got a new dress, and I had my hair done. Sophie did my nails. I'm not letting all this go to waste."

His hand moved to my knee before trailing slowly up my thigh. He raised an eyebrow. "I wasn't planning on letting it go to waste."

6

"Brian!"

He silenced me with a kiss. I moaned as his hand worked its way higher up my thigh.

"No!" I pushed him away. "Nice try."

"Come on." His mouth moved to my neck. "Surely it's more tempting to stay at home."

"It's tempting," I said with a sigh. "But no! Get off me." I pushed him away again. Where I found the willpower for that I've no idea. "I want to go to the party. Please."

"Fine." He leaned back against the sideboard. "It's boring though."

"It can't be," I said. Brian worked for an investment bank. I'd never worked in a corporate environment so I'd never been to a proper office party. I'd seen them on TV though and they were always fun. "We'll have a great time."

Brian checked his watch. "It doesn't start for hours, you know?"

"We can go for dinner first."

He took a deep breath. "Okay, but I need a shower." He gave me a quick peck then rolled his eyes. "The things I do for you."

It was a party for goodness sake. I've no idea why he made it sound like he was doing me a huge favour.

"Thank you," I called as he made for the stairs.

HANNAH ELLIS

Chapter 2

I was a little disappointed that the office Christmas party wasn't held in the office. I'm not sure why. Brian said it would be ridiculous. Who would want to go back to work after work? He had a point I suppose. And the hotel in town was a pleasant enough venue.

The large function room was decked out very nicely. There was a bar, a buffet, a dance floor. Waiters wandering with champagne and canapés. It had it all really.

"I can't believe you dragged me here," Brian whispered when we walked in.

"It'll be so much fun." I squeezed his arm. My eye was drawn to a woman nearby. She was tall with beautiful long blonde hair. Her backless dress was stunning in a gorgeous shade of teal. All flowy and sophisticated. She looked like a model. So did the other stick-like creature she was talking to. *Oh, my god.* I thought Brian worked in banking not in the modelling industry.

"Am I dressed okay?" I asked.

"Of course. You look great. Why?"

Because I felt frumpy, that was why. I'd been so happy with my little black dress, but suddenly I felt very conservative and boring. I took a glass of fizz from the waiter who appeared in front of us. Quickly,

I clinked my glass against Brian's and gulped at it.

"You okay?" Brian asked.

I nodded and we were interrupted by a guy who slapped Brian on the back.

"How's that merger of yours coming on?" he asked with a grin. "You ever going to close the deal?"

Brian smiled tightly and rested his hand on the small of my back. "This is my fiancée, Marie."

The corners of my mouth twitched as he called me his fiancée. I wasn't sure I'd ever get used to that.

"This is Greg," Brian said, as I shook the guy's hand.

"Nice to meet you," we said at once.

"Brian's finally showing you off then is he?" He laughed loudly. "We weren't sure if he'd made you up. Either that or you were twice his age or ugly as hell."

"We were just heading to the buffet," Brian said, slapping his shoulder. "Catch you later, Greg."

"Interesting character," I said as we wandered away. That was me being polite.

"He's a complete idiot," Brian said.

"I'm not actually hungry." I gave the buffet table a cursory glance. We'd been out to a lovely little Italian restaurant before the party.

"Me neither," Brian said. "I just wanted to get away from Greg."

"Brian!" Another middle-aged man came and shook his hand. "How are things looking with the Sullivan account now? That's been a bloody nightmare, hasn't it?"

Brian nodded slowly. "It's not been the smoothest of projects. This is my fiancée, Marie."

"Mike Shepherd," he said extending his hand and grinning. "Great to meet you."

"You too." I smiled.

"I don't know how you got the missus to come," he said as though I wasn't there. "Mine refuses point blank. Not that I mind." He nodded in the direction of the two model-like women.

"We were just going to grab some food," Brian said. "Talk to you later."

"Are we going to end up circling the buffet table all night?" I asked quietly.

"I told you it'd be boring."

"It's not quite what I was expecting," I admitted.

"I didn't think you were coming." A gorgeous brunette put a hand on Brian's shoulder and kissed his cheek. My hand automatically formed a fist. She was a bit older and looked quite intimidating in her cream trouser suit.

"You must be Marie?" She held a hand out to me.

"That's me." I don't know why I adopted a silly voice.

"It's good to put a face to the name," she said.

She waved to someone across the room and waltzed off again before I even caught her name.

"Matt!" Brian called as a younger looking guy crossed the room. He came over and shook Brian's hand.

"I thought you said you never come to these things?"

"Marie dragged me along." He nodded in my direction and the guy leaned in to kiss my cheek.

"I'm Matt," he said warmly. "You'll learn your lesson about work parties."

11

"I didn't realise everyone would talk about work," I said.

"It's crazy, isn't it?" He scratched his jaw. "I just came to take advantage of the free bar before I head off for a night on the town."

"Good idea," I said. "I thought it would be wild and crazy, but it's quite sedate really."

"Here's what I do," Matt said. "Anytime anyone says merger, you take a drink. Or account or acquisition … anything to do with business really, you take a sip of your drink. It makes conversations much more entertaining."

"I like it." I nodded my head in approval.

Brian shot me a warning glance. I suppose he didn't want me to get drunk and show him up.

An older guy arrived and shook Brian's hand, then Matt's before turning to me.

"Carl Thompson," he said.

Why did everyone introduce themselves using their full name? I had trouble remembering one name, never mind two.

"Marie," I said, shaking his hand. He probably thought I was very weird. Like a big celebrity who only went by one name.

"Any progress with the Sullivan account?" he said, turning to Brian. I caught Matt's eye and took a sip of my drink.

"Still in discussions," Brian said.

"I thought it would be a straightforward deal for you there. They've got the backers and capital doesn't seem to be an issue …"

I gulped my drink until it was empty, then got myself a fresh one when the waiter came past. I stifled a giggle as I neared the bottom of that glass. Matt's drinking game was lethal. Someone needed to shut Carl Thompson up before I drank all the champagne.

"Sorry, Carl." Brian interrupted him. "We were actually just about to get food."

"You do that." He grinned and wandered away. Matt and I looked at each other and laughed.

"You just downed two glasses of wine," Brian said with raised eyebrows.

"A glass and a half," I corrected him. "And it was champagne. It was that guy's fault for waffling on about work!"

"I'm done," Matt said. "I can't take this lame excuse for a party any longer. Have a good night!" He was chuckling as he wandered away.

"Can we leave yet?" Brian asked.

"I thought it would be fun." My shoulders slouched as my eyes roamed the room. It really was a terrible excuse for a party.

"I did try to tell you."

"I believe you now. Can't really believe I passed up your hand on my thigh for this."

He laughed. "You're drunk."

"I really liked the hand on my thigh move." I hiccupped and swayed slightly. "Did you feel rejected?"

He rolled his eyes. "I think I might take you home now."

"Good." I leaned in and nuzzled his neck. "We'll go with your plan for the evening instead."

"You are *so* drunk." He took my arm. We were halfway across the room when a group of men called him over.

"One minute," he said to me.

There was no way I was going to nod and smile along to anymore boring business chat. "I'll get another drink," I said, edging away from him.

Typical. There were no waiters around when you needed them. I headed for the bar instead.

"I'll have a glass of wine," I said to the barman. "Actually, make it a shot of tequila." There was an old guy sitting alone at the end of the bar. His tie was loose and he was nursing what looked to be whiskey. "Tequila makes me happy," I said to him. "You look like you could do with one too. Have you ever been to a more miserable party? Thank god there's free booze, that's all I can say." He stared at me. "Make it two," I said to the barman.

"I don't drink tequila," the old guy said when I pushed it down the bar to him.

I pointed my shot glass at him. "You should. It'll cheer you up." I downed my drink, but he didn't touch his.

"I don't recognise you," he said. "Do you work for the firm?"

"No. Thank god. What a boring bunch. I'm with Brian. He's my fiancé." I flashed my ring to prove it. Then I glanced over at Brian. "Oh, my god. I only left him for two minutes. They're like vultures." There were two beautiful women, standing one either side of him. One had her hand on his arm. Apparently he'd said something hilarious because they were both laughing away. "Who does the hiring at this place? Someone with an eye for the ladies, obviously."

"I'm fairly sure they have to employ people based on qualifications and experience."

"Yes. The good old days of being able to sleep your way to the top are long gone." I lifted the empty shot glass to the barman, indicating my need for another. I chuckled and turned to the old guy. "That was a joke, by the way. I'm all for equality." I scanned the room. "Why are they all so bloody beautiful though? Is it a money thing? Everyone's rich enough to make themselves look good? How many nose jobs do you reckon there are in the room?"

He stared at me and didn't indulge in my game of spot the nose job.

"What's so bad about the party?" he asked.

"I don't know. I pictured it differently. I thought there'd be that one person who gets totally sloshed and embarrasses themself. And I thought there'd be some sort of office romance. You know, someone nipping off to the stockroom for a quickie and stumbling back out with their buttons done up wrong." I sighed and leaned on the bar. "That's the sort of thing I was expecting. Everyone here's talking about work."

"Maybe it's because it's in a hotel," he said. "No one's nipping off for a fumble in a cupboard when there are perfectly good bedrooms upstairs."

I laughed. "That's a good point. This hotel's too classy for an office party, that's the problem. They should just have had it in the office. Start handing out tequila at the end of the work day and go from there."

"It is pretty dull," he said.

"Everyone needs to loosen up." I stood and walked over to him. "Look how tense you are …" I gave his shoulders a quick rub, then nudged the tequila closer to him and reached for my shot. I held the glass up until he joined me and we downed them in unison.

"You know what the worst thing is?" I sat on the barstool again and lowered my voice. "I passed up sex for this." I raised an eyebrow and nodded. "Brian didn't want to come. He was trying to convince me to stay at home …" I wobbled on my stool and laughed.

"Sorry." Brian appeared, hovering over me. "I kept getting dragged into conversations."

"No problem." I leaned my head back onto his chest. "I was just telling this nice gentleman about you putting your hand up my dress."

I felt Brian tense. He moved and extended his hand to my friend.

"Mr Clifford," he said curtly.

"Brian." He nodded. "Your fiancée's been giving me some tips on how to liven up the party next year."

"I'm sure she has."

My new friend stood and patted Brian on the shoulder. "I think I'll call it a night. You two have fun."

Brian smiled tightly until he'd disappeared from sight. Then he slumped onto the bar beside me.

"Did you really just tell my boss about me groping you in the kitchen?"

I bit down on my bottom lip. "That's your boss?"

He nodded. "He's the Managing Director."

"Oh, my god." My hand shot to my mouth. "The thing I said about my dress might not even be the worst thing I said to him." I gasped as I thought back on the conversation. "I massaged his shoulders!"

Brian tipped his head back and groaned. "Can we please go now?"

"Yeah," I said sheepishly.

He took my hand and led me straight to the door. There were a couple in the foyer who Brian smiled at and veered me away from. "Don't speak to anyone," he whispered.

Outside, I pulled my coat around me.

"I'm so sorry," I said squeezing Brian's hand.

"Don't worry about it." He was peering down the road looking for a taxi.

"I can't believe I made you go to your Christmas party and I completely embarrassed you."

"You didn't. It's fine."

I dropped his hand and he finally looked at me.

"I really am sorry."

He narrowed his eyes. "It doesn't matter."

"But you just told me not to talk to anyone. You can't even trust me to open my mouth."

"I didn't mean it like that," he said. "I didn't want to get stuck chatting to anyone else. They're all so boring."

"I honestly thought it would be fun. I thought people would be dancing and having a laugh. And I thought I could make friends with your colleagues so I'd know who you're talking about when you tell me about work stuff."

He shook his head. "It's not that sort of party."

"I realise that now. I didn't even know what anyone was talking about. The only conversation I managed to have was a really inappropriate one. You should just keep me hidden away at home."

"No chance." He smiled and took my face in his hands to kiss me.

"I'm sorry. I really didn't mean to embarrass you."

He frowned and kissed the side of my head, then

he took my hand and pulled me back inside the hotel.

"What are you doing?"

"You're right," he said. "What kind of party is it if no one dances?"

I shook my head and pulled on his arm. "We can't dance, Brian. No one's dancing!"

When we reached the sedate function room Brian flung his jacket on a chair and took mine from me.

"We're not really going to dance are we?" I said.

"Someone needs to get the party going!"

I laughed as he pulled me onto the dance floor and lifted my arm over my head to twirl me around.

"*You're* embarrassing *me* now," I said.

"You love it." He twirled me again. Thankfully another couple joined us on the dance floor, and then a few more people.

"I told you we could liven things up," he said.

"Shall I get everyone a shot of tequila?"

"What is this obsession with tequila?"

"It makes me happy!"

He rolled his eyes, then leaned down to kiss me. When he kept kissing me, I eventually pushed him away, laughing. "What are you doing?"

He licked his lips. "I thought I'd snog your face off in the middle of the dance floor until someone told us to get a room. It'll give people something to gossip about on Monday."

"I feel like my craziness might be rubbing off on you! Let's go home."

He smiled as I led him off the dance floor. "It was just starting to get fun."

Chapter 3

Amazingly, I managed to get up before Brian on Saturday and sneaked downstairs to make him breakfast in bed.

"Good morning," I whispered, setting the bacon sandwich and cup of coffee on the bedside table.

"Morning." He blinked me into focus and smiled lazily. "What's going on?"

"I made you breakfast," I said perching on the edge of the bed.

He sat up and reached for the coffee. "Is it my birthday?"

"No. I just wanted to do something nice."

He raised an eyebrow. "Why?"

"Can't I just do something nice?" Climbing over him, I crawled back under the covers at my side of the bed. My head wasn't feeling brilliant after all the alcohol the previous night.

Brian took a bite of his sandwich and stared at me.

"I feel guilty about last night," I said sheepishly.

"Next time you might listen to me when I say I don't want to go."

"I don't feel bad about making you go. Just about getting drunk and embarrassing you in front of your boss."

He shrugged. "I'm sure he's heard worse."

"I don't really fit in with your work friends, do I?"

"No." He laughed. "Thank god. And they're not friends; they're colleagues."

"You work with some very beautiful women," I remarked. Brian didn't comment, just tucked into his sandwich. "And your boss said they employ people based on qualifications and stuff so they're not airheads either."

"I can see what you're thinking." Brian put his plate aside and lay down, facing me. "You're wondering why I'm slumming it with you when I'm surrounded by intelligent, beautiful women at work. I could probably have my pick of them."

I slapped his chest and a grin broke over his face. His hands found my waist under the covers and he pulled me to him. "Don't get all insecure and needy. It doesn't suit you."

"Sorry." It was hard not feel a little inadequate after seeing the women he worked with.

He pushed my hair from my face. "After all, you might be brainless and ugly but you make a mean bacon sandwich."

I smiled proudly. "That's true."

"I love you," he said, dotting kisses along my jaw.

"I love you too. Shall I cancel on Linda and we can stay in bed all day?"

"Tempting," he said. "But I've got some work to do."

"Okay." I didn't really want to cancel on Linda anyway. We always went out for lunch on Saturdays and had a walk around the shops. She was in her fifties and had become like a second mother to me. I enjoyed our Saturday afternoon outings.

"Are we going to your mum's tomorrow?" Brian asked.

"Yes." That was another regular occurrence. Sunday lunch with my mum and aunt. My weekends really were a riot. At least I had Brian to come with me to my mum's now. It made it much more bearable.

Dragging myself from the cosy bed, I got dressed and waited for Linda to pick me up. I was surprised to see Sophie in the car too. The three of us had met by chance at a bizarre excuse for a slimming club. Sophie and I hadn't intended to be there. We just got lost looking for a speed dating evening.

Anyway, we'd somehow ended up friends. There was Jake too; he was the only one of who'd actually been trying to lose weight. I still affectionately referred to them as my fat club friends, and we still met on Thursday evenings, which was when the original slimming club took place.

Sophie was nineteen and a feisty character who kept us all on our toes. She'd ended up being a great friend. It was her who'd done my nails for the party and helped me decide what to wear.

"What are you doing here?" I asked as I climbed into the car. Usually, it was only Linda and me on Saturdays.

"I thought I'd come and get the gossip from the party," she said. "I didn't like the thought of Linda hearing it before me."

"My head still hurts so talk quietly please. Linda, do you mind if we skip shopping today? I don't have the energy."

"Of course." She patted my knee. "I was expecting you might want to just go for lunch."

21

"Perfect."

She drove us to her favourite tearoom and we ordered afternoon tea to share. It was so cute with all the little sandwiches and cakes neatly arranged on the three-tiered cake stand.

"Tell us about last night then," Sophie said as she bit into a scone with jam and cream.

"It wasn't as much fun as I expected." I gave them a quick rundown of the evening from how Brian didn't want to go, to my embarrassing chat with his boss. I also mentioned how attractive all the women were.

"I can't believe you're jealous of the women Brian works with," Sophie said. "That's pathetic."

"I'm not jealous. I was just surprised that they're all so perfect-looking."

"You're jealous," she insisted. "I'm surprised at you. I didn't have you down as the crazy jealous girlfriend."

"I'm not!" I laughed and Sophie gave me a knowing look.

"At least you got to dance," Linda said kindly.

"Brian only danced with me so I wouldn't feel so bad about embarrassing him."

"I'm sure you didn't embarrass him," Linda said.

Sophie wiped crumbs from her mouth. "Telling his boss about your sex life is a little embarrassing."

I chuckled. "Poor Brian."

"It's sounds like it was probably the most interesting conversation his boss's had in a while," Sophie said. "They all sound stuck-up and boring."

"It made me realise, I don't really know anything about Brian's job. He never talks to me about work."

"Sounds like that's a good thing," Sophie said.

"He probably doesn't want to bother you with it," Linda said.

"Or he thinks I wouldn't understand it." To be fair, all that financial talk went way over my head.

"Why do you even care?" Sophie said.

I shrugged. "I don't know really."

"Let's talk Christmas," Sophie said, changing the subject abruptly. "I'm going to book you in to the spa for a day of pampering. A little pre-Christmas treat for you both." Sophie worked at a health spa attached to a wellness hotel and had often talked about Linda and me going for some treatments.

"I don't think it's really my thing," Linda said. "I've never done anything like that."

"You'll love it," Sophie said. "I can do all your treatments. You don't need to worry. I'll look after you."

I nodded my vague agreement. It might be fun.

"I want you all to come to a carol service at my church," Linda said. "It's on Christmas Eve."

"No chance," Sophie said. "I'm not spending Christmas Eve on a hard pew, listening to someone preach at me."

"It's a carol service," Linda said patiently. "You'll enjoy it. It's wonderful. Singing all the Christmas carols puts you in the Christmas spirit."

"Vodka will be my spirit of choice," Sophie said. "I already told Jeff we're going to the pub on Christmas Eve."

"How is Jeff?" I asked. He and Sophie had been dating for about six months. We all knew Jeff from the hotel where the original fat club was held. He worked on reception and it'd been Jeff who'd sent Sophie and me into the wrong room when we wanted to go speed dating.

"He's fine," Sophie said flatly. They'd definitely gone through the honeymoon period and were out the other side. She grumbled about him a lot.

"What are you doing on Christmas Day?" Linda asked me when Sophie didn't say anymore.

"We've got my mum and Aunt Kath coming over for Christmas dinner. Other than that it will be quiet. Just Brian and me. I'm looking forward to it."

"That sounds nice," Linda said. "Ours will just be me and George, as always."

"You know Christmas is on a Thursday?" Sophie said. "What's happening with fat club?"

I chuckled and rolled my eyes. "Nothing is happening with fat club. Obviously. It's Christmas."

"Hmm." Sophie flashed me a mischievous grin. It made me nervous. Surely they wouldn't all turn up for fat club on Christmas Day? I wouldn't put it past them.

"How are the wedding plans?" Linda asked.

"On hold," I said. "I'll think about it properly in the new year. There's too much going on at the moment to start planning a wedding."

"I can't wait." Linda hunched her shoulders up. "It'll be magical whatever you do."

We sat for almost two hours, picking at the yummy food and chatting away. I was glad we'd skipped shopping.

When Linda dropped me at home, I heard Brian on the phone as soon as I walked in. I listened at the kitchen doorway. It was a work call.

Putting my head round the door, I smiled and intended to leave him to it.

"Hang on. She just walked in." He held the phone out to me. "It's Grace."

My best friend Grace worked for the same company as Brian. They'd worked in the same building before Grace and her boyfriend relocated to the New York branch.

"Hi!" I said, smiling into the phone. "How are you?"

"Fine," she said. "Busy as always. We're not going to make it back over for Christmas. I was hoping we might but it'll be too much of a rush."

"That's a shame." I'd never been under the impression they would make it back so I wasn't overly disappointed.

"Poor Brian," she said. "Sounds like he's having a rough time at work."

"Yeah," I agreed vaguely. He'd moved to the dining room and was hunched over his laptop.

"Christmas will be a good break for him," she said. "How's everything with you?"

"All fine." I hopped up to perch on a barstool. "We went to the Christmas party last night. Brian's work do."

"He told me." She laughed. "I can't believe you convinced him to go. Those things are awful."

"Yeah, it was pretty bad."

"Brian said it was fun in the end anyway."

I smiled. That was pretty generous of him.

"Sorry," Grace said, sounding suddenly distracted. "I'm going to have to go. I just wanted to let you know about Christmas. I'll call for a proper catch up soon. I want to hear all your wedding plans!"

"That will be a short conversation," I said dryly.

She chuckled. "Talk soon."

"Bye!" I ended the call and wandered into the dining room. "You okay?" I rubbed Brian's shoulders.

"Yeah." He leaned back, stretching his neck and sighing.

"You can talk to me about work, you know?"

"I'd rather not," he said. "It's boring."

I continued kneading his shoulders. He'd talk to Grace about work, but not me. It seemed a silly thing to feel left out about.

"Guess what?" He pushed his chair back and pulled me onto his lap.

"What?" I grinned.

"I went and bought a Christmas tree."

I smiled, delighted, and shot off to the living room in search of it.

"I had some decorations up in the loft," Brian said. "But we might need to get more."

"It's so exciting." I dived into his box of decorations and got straight to work. The afternoon flew by and the living room looked lovely when we snuggled up on the couch that evening. The tree was all lit up and there was a string of fairy lights around the window too. Brian got the fire going and it felt wonderfully cosy.

"I'm really excited about Christmas now," I said.

"Me too." Brian hugged me tighter.

"Our first Christmas together," I said. "It's going to be so lovely. Just you and me cuddled up like this. That's all I need."

Chapter 4

My Aunt Kath cooked roast chicken for us on Sunday. I was always happy she cooked for us at Mum's house. My mum was slightly eccentric and her forays into cooking tended to display that fact quite clearly. She'd been known to serve me up such monstrosities as spaghetti with Nutella, lasagne with sardines, carrot cake with added peas. The list was long and ridiculous.

"That was delicious," I said to Aunt Kath as I finished my lunch.

"It was," Brian agreed. "Thanks."

"I was thinking about Christmas," Mum said. "Do you want me to cook lunch?"

"No. It's fine," I said quickly, catching the look of panic on Aunt Kath's face. "I already said we'd do it at Brian's place." He flashed me a knowing look. "*Our* place," I corrected myself. "I'm happy to cook."

"I'm looking after Rex though," Mum said.

"You're welcome to bring the dog," I said. Mum had a job as a dog walker and she seemed to look after one little dog most of the time. Rex was snoozing in a dog basket at the side of the room while we ate. He kept opening his eyes and looking at us, clearly trying to suss out whether he might get thrown some scraps. At least Mum had him well trained and he wasn't begging at the table.

"Are you sure that's okay?" Mum asked.

"Yes." Brian and I said at once. Anything to avoid my mum cooking Christmas dinner.

"We put the decorations up yesterday," I said. "I'm starting to feel very Christmassy."

"I should get mine up," Mum said. There was a look of panic in her eyes; like she might get up and do it there and then. Thankfully, she only got up to clear the table. We all helped with the tidying up and it was done in no time. Aunt Kath put the kettle on.

"Have you set a date for the wedding yet?" Mum asked as we lingered in the kitchen. She asked this every time we saw her.

"Not yet," I said, rolling my eyes.

"I thought we had a deal," Brian said, slinging an arm around my shoulders, then looking at Mum. "You said you'd stop nagging me if I proposed."

I elbowed him in the ribs and Mum laughed.

"No," she said. "I'm going to nag you about the wedding now, and after that I'll nag you about grandchildren."

That was quite witty for Mum. There was a twinkle in her eye. She often made us laugh but she rarely intended to.

"Well," she said. "I'll need to make cushions for them." She was back to being serious. Homemade cushions were her speciality. She knitted pictures on the front of them. She made them for every occasion.

"I think you've got some time," Brian said with a grin.

"I don't know what colours," she said. "Or I could get started."

"Make a variety," I suggested. "Or just do white or yellow. Neutral colours."

"Marie!" Brian shot me a look and wandered into the living room.

"What?" I followed him and curled up in his lap when he sat in the armchair.

"Were you seriously just encouraging your mum to make cushions for our unborn children?"

"It's good to be prepared," I said.

We hadn't really talked about kids but I was certain Brian would want children.

"How many cushions should I tell her to make?" I asked cheekily.

He looked thoughtful. "Two?"

"Two's good."

"Three would be fine too," he said.

I frowned. "I'll tell her two for now."

"I can't believe you're encouraging her."

"Anything to get her to stop going on about the flipping wedding."

He sighed and leaned his head on me.

"Are you okay?" I ran my thumb back and forth across the back of his neck.

"Yes. Work's just been stressing me out."

I planted a kiss on his head. "It'll soon be Christmas."

Chapter 5

"There you are!" Anne said when I arrived at work on Monday morning. She was my constantly cheerful co-worker at the small travel agent. The cheerfulness was annoying but she was generally fun to work with. She was in her fifties and was quite entertaining in her own way.

I glanced at my watch. "I'm not late, am I?"

"No. But we were just talking about you."

I raised my eyebrows at Jason, who was sitting in my chair.

"Move," I said, shooing him away. "That's an interesting clothing ensemble," I told him as he got out of my way.

Jason was a new friend of ours. I use the term 'friend' very loosely. One day, he'd come in to book a holiday and he and Anne had hit it off so he was a regular visitor to the shop now. He often called in between clients.

He was a personal trainer, which was why I was reluctant to call him a friend. Anyone that took exercise so seriously was slightly off balance in my opinion. He was another happy character too so I really struggled to relate to him. I presumed the cheerful façade was a cover for some deep-rooted issues, and he was actually miserable on the inside.

"What's wrong with my outfit?" he asked as he began doing star jumps in the middle of the room. He never stayed still for long.

Jason was well over six feet tall and dominated the room as he jumped away. He was wearing short shorts and long socks with a stylish but too tight purple hoodie. He also wore a sweatband around his forehead and should look ridiculous. There was something about him though; he was so manly and good-looking that he somehow managed to pull off his slightly odd clothing ensemble.

"Nothing," I said, not wanting to get into it. "Aren't you cold though? It's December."

"I keep moving." He jumped, splaying out his arms and legs. "So I keep warm."

"We want to hear about the Christmas party," Anne said eagerly. She handed me a cup of coffee and I thanked her as I wrapped my hands around the steaming mug.

"It was a disaster," I said with a shrug.

"Why?" Anne asked.

"I drank too much and started telling Brian's boss about our sex life."

Jason stopped his jumping to laugh.

"You didn't really, did you?" Anne asked.

"Yeah." I nodded. "I sort of did."

Anne tutted and shook her head. "Apart from that, how was it?"

"A bunch of stuck-up people talking about work. Quite boring really. Plus, all the women are stick thin and beautiful so I felt quite self-conscious."

Jason grinned. "You know what you need?"

"If you say personal trainer, I'll come and show

you my boxing moves. That'd be a good bit of exercise for me."

"Oh, come on." His shoulders slumped and he stuck his bottom lip out.

"No," I said adamantly. "We tried that nonsense before, remember? I ended up hopping on a bus to get away from you?" He'd insisted on giving me a free fitness session when we first met, but it didn't really go well.

"But you were my most fun client. And it would be great for your self-esteem."

"There's nothing wrong with my self-esteem."

"No. Nothing at all. Until you see the hotties who work with your fiancé."

"Well, thankfully Brian loves me for my sparkling personality so it's fine."

"I'd do it for free," he said.

That definitely made it more appealing. "Would you?" I asked, blowing out a breath and surprising myself by actually considering the idea.

"No!" he said fiercely. "Of course not. I'm a trained professional. Don't disrespect me by expecting freebies. You already had your free trial."

"Mates' rates though," I said.

"I'll give you a five per cent discount."

"Five per cent? Are we even friends?"

"Fine. Ten per cent. Final offer."

"I can't do it anyway," I said. "Brian was already a bit funny when I mentioned the women at work. He doesn't like me being insecure. If I tell him I've got a personal trainer, he'll really think I've got issues."

"It's not about him," Jason said.

Anne nodded her agreement. "It's about your

health and feeling good about yourself." She looked to Jason. He grinned. He'd trained her well.

"Brian won't believe that. He'll say I'm worrying about nothing."

"I've got some time free in the afternoons." Jason got his Blackberry out and tapped away in his calendar. "We could do a couple of sessions straight after work. We can jog home and then do a short workout at your place."

"Well, you've just made the bus journey home seem like a luxury." I sighed. It probably wasn't a bad idea to add some exercise into my life. And if I did it straight from work, I wouldn't even need to mention it to Brian. He always came home later than me.

"How about Tuesdays and Fridays?"

"Not Fridays," I said. "I'm not exercising at the weekend."

"Friday's not the weekend."

My eyes widened at his idiotic comment. "It's the weekend as soon as I walk out of that door on Friday. There is no point in you arguing otherwise."

"Fine. Tuesdays and Thursdays."

I took a deep breath. "Okay. Not tomorrow though, I need time to psyche myself up."

"We'll start on Thursday." He checked his watch. "I've gotta run."

"He's a funny one, isn't he?" Anne said after he left. "Brightens the place up."

I'm fairly sure I could've been offended by that remark. But I was too busy pondering what had just happened.

"Did I really just agree to two personal training sessions a week?"

"It'll be fun," Anne said cheerfully.
That would depend on your idea of fun, I suppose.

HANNAH ELLIS

Chapter 6

Thursday came around far too quick. Jason arrived at five o'clock on the dot.

"I've changed my mind," I said. "You caught me in a moment of weakness on Monday."

"Fine." He took a seat in the chair opposite me and smiled sweetly. He was up to something. No way he'd give up that easily.

"Haven't you got something else to be doing then?" I switched off my computer and reached for my bag. For some reason, I'd actually brought a backpack with some vaguely suitable workout attire. Carrying that to and from work was enough exercise for me.

"Nothing to do," Jason said casually. "You booked me for the hour. Last minute cancellations are quite nice actually. I get an hour off and still get paid."

"I'm not paying you!"

"You booked me for an hour. I need twenty-four hours notice if you want to cancel, otherwise you still need to pay. That's how it works I'm afraid."

My jaw was clamped but I managed a tight smile. "Wait there," I growled.

I could hear him and Anne chuckling as I went to change in the small bathroom.

"You need to warm up," he said as I ran past him

and out of the shop door. I called goodbye to Anne as I went.

"I'm not warming up in the middle of the shop," I said.

"We can warm up here."

I glanced around the busy shopping street. Was he mad? I couldn't even dignify the comment with a response. Also, breathing was becoming hard work and I was fairly sure I couldn't speak. The good thing about such a populated area was that I ran faster. I hated the idea of people watching me. I whizzed by as quickly as possible. We were out of the main part of town before I knew it. I was about to collapse and die, but at least there wouldn't be many witnesses.

In the park, I stopped; panting and resting on my knees. Taking deep breaths, I stumbled to a nearby bench.

"Remind me why I'm doing this?"

Jason crouched in front of me and picked up my left foot, gently rotating my ankle. It felt quite nice actually. "It's good for you," he said.

"You say that." I was still puffing and panting. "But so far it's made me feel terrible. I might throw up." I threw my head back and tried to control my breathing.

"That's a sign you need to do more. Jogging for ten minutes shouldn't make you need to vomit."

"It obviously doesn't agree with me."

He glanced around the park. "We could do the workout on the grass, since the weather's decent. Then jog home." He pulled a water bottle from his backpack and handed it to me. I gulped greedily.

"The grass is wet," I said.

"I've got mats." He pulled them from his backpack with a flourish.

I followed him over to the grass and flopped onto the mat when he laid it out for me.

Unfortunately, he then set himself up beside me and began lifting his legs in the air and insisting I do the same. It was torture. And I was paying for it. What had my life come to?

"That'll do," I said after one stomach crunch too many. "Let's just go."

"We've hardly started." He jumped up when I dragged myself off the ground.

"How about some star jumps?"

"How about you don't push your luck! I'll jog home. That's it."

He sighed and I set off up the hill while he put the mats away in his backpack. It only took him a few seconds to catch me up.

"I'll let you ease into it," he said. "We'll build up to the full hour."

I might have had something to say about that but I'd lost the power of speech again. My lungs really didn't like me running.

Jason stared at the house when we finally made it back. I leaned on the front wall, gasping for breath.

"You live here?" he asked.

I nodded vigorously.

"Wow."

"Rich boyfriend," I said with a grin.

He raised his hand and I managed a limp high-five.

"This was fun." I slowly walked up the front steps. "I'll cancel Tuesday's session now to save me the cancellation fee. In fact, why don't we cancel all future sessions?"

"No." He went all whiney and wide-eyed. "This is good for you. After the first few sessions it'll get easier, I promise."

"Are you stuck for business or something? I could help you with promotional material, or write you a recommendation."

"I've got loads of business," he said. "I had an influx of footballers wives and minor celebrities. They're all a bit annoying though. You'd be my down-to-earth client. We have a laugh."

I sighed. I *was* a lot of fun. "I'll give it a few more sessions but I can't promise much more than that."

He grinned.

"See you next week then," I said, drearily.

"Can I come in and fill up my water bottle?"

"You just want to nosey at the house, don't you?"

"And I need water." He held his bottle upside down to back up his claim.

I beckoned him in with a flick of the head. He looked around with wide eyes as I led him down the hall to the kitchen.

"It's gorgeous," he said.

"It is, isn't it?" I hopped up onto a barstool and he leaned against the counter. "Got anything fun planned for the weekend?" I asked.

"Nothing definite. I usually find a party or something on Saturday night."

"Have you got a girlfriend?" I'm not sure why I suddenly felt comfortable prying into his private life. Probably due to the way he was sizing up my kitchen.

He bobbed his head in an ambiguous gesture. "Nothing serious. I like to keep my options open." He filled his bottle under the tap. "Can I hang around and meet Brian? I'm intrigued."

"No. He thinks I'm crazy enough as it is. If he finds out I've started exercising, he'll really think I've lost the plot."

Jason snorted a laugh.

"Besides, he won't be home for ages. I might need a nap after an hour of you torturing me."

"It was half an hour," he said, frowning.

"Felt like longer." I slipped off the stool and walked him back to the door.

"See you next week," he called and took off at a run. What a nutter.

After a quick shower, I was about to put my pyjamas on and then remembered it was Thursday. Fat club evening. I got dressed and waited for Brian to get home. He was late, and came in shortly after seven looking flustered.

"Sorry." He gave me a quick kiss. "Are you ready to go?"

"They're supposed to be coming here," I said.

"That's not going to happen. Get your coat on."

I reached for my coat on the rack. "I thought I was very firm last week. We can't keep meeting at Grace's house now that I've moved out. It's practically trespassing."

"They're creatures of habit," Brian said. "Besides, I think Grace is happy someone's keeping an eye on the place."

"She might want to rent it out soon. They're like Thursday night squatters."

"I'm sure they'll stop if someone moves in. Grace doesn't want to rent it at the moment anyway. Not until she decided how long they're staying in New York."

I climbed into the car and waited for Brian to get in. "I need to get the spare key back from Sophie." That was the problem: Sophie had a key for my best friend's house from when she lived there with me for a while.

"I hate to break it to you," Brian said. "They've all got keys."

"Really?"

He nodded. "Sophie got extras cut so whoever gets there first can let themselves in."

I threw my hands up. "They're ridiculous!"

He laughed and started the car. It was only a five-minute drive and I could hear the chatter from my fat club gang as soon as I opened the door.

"You're late!" Sophie shouted.

"You're in the wrong house," I called back. "I keep telling you we should meet at Brian's place." I caught myself. "*Our* place."

"Whatever." Sophie was grinning at me when I walked into the living room. She gave me a quick hug then moved to Brian. I was fairly gobsmacked when she put her hands on his cheeks and gave him a big kiss on the lips. Brian raised his eyebrows, then looked at me and flopped into the armchair. Our fat club friends were slightly quirky. Sometimes, it was best just not to ask.

Sophie casually perched herself on the arm of the armchair and dangled her feet in Brian's lap. I opened my mouth to say something, then realised she was probably only doing it for some kind of reaction. Definitely better to ignore her. I took a seat on the couch with Jake and Linda.

"We've just been discussing Christmas," Jake said.

"It's on a Thursday, you know?" Sophie said with a sweet little smile.

"No." I glared at Sophie. "Whatever you're thinking, the answer is no!"

Chapter 7

"I'm sorry but it's not going to happen." I rolled my eyes at the ridiculous idea. "I don't care what day Christmas is on, we're not having fat club on Christmas Day."

"So you're going to abandon us at Christmas?" Sophie's eyes sparkled with mischief. "Just ditch your closest friends on the one day of the year when people are supposed to come together?"

I took a deep breath and tried to keep my emotions under control.

"Christmas is a time for families," I said. "Surely everyone will be with their families." I looked from Jake to Linda, hoping they'd back me up. Sophie was just trying to wind me up again.

"Well, to be fair," Jake said. "We've not missed a Thursday yet. That's quite a streak we've got going. For me, Thursdays means fat club. I'm not sure I'm willing to give it up for Christmas. As you've rightly pointed out, Christmas is about family so we'd need to bring our nearest and dearest, but I think that would be okay, just this once."

"I'd have to bring George," Linda put in quietly, referring to her husband. Linda's smile was so angelic it was hard to say no to. However, on this occasion, I was going to have to.

"No!"

A row of big puppy dog eyes pleaded with me but I wasn't going to give in. I already had my Christmas planned and it didn't involve fat club. I would stand my ground and make them see reason even if it took me all night, which I was fairly sure it would.

"I'm sorry, Linda," I said. "Don't start crying. It's nothing against George, or you. It's just that I have a very traditional Christmas and it's important for me to keep up the traditions of my family ..." I trailed off, hearing how ridiculous I sounded. I looked round to see if anyone was buying the nonsense that was falling out of my mouth. They clearly weren't. All I wanted was a quiet Christmas with Brian. I couldn't say that though. They'd no doubt accuse me of being selfish. I'd try a different tack with them.

"Also I think having fat club on Christmas Day would be really inappropriate. Christmas is about stuffing yourself full of food all day long. And you want us to sit and chat about healthy eating and weigh poor old Jake? You're a cruel bunch. Jake deserves a day off." I gave them the big eyes now. Let's see how they liked it.

Sophie started the giggling and the rest of them joined in.

"Who even knows where the weighing scales are?" Jake asked.

"I do!" I stuck a hand under the couch but came up empty handed. Lying down on the floor, I peered under, shoving Linda's stockinged feet to one side. There was nothing there. I pulled myself back up to sitting. "What have you done with them?"

"I took them home months ago," Jake said.

Okay, so admittedly we hadn't had a weigh-in for a while and in all honesty it was a bit odd that we still referred to our Thursday evening get-togethers as fat club.

Jake was the only one of us who actually ever had any weight issues and it turned out all he needed was a boyfriend to cook healthy food for him. I think Jake only knew how to cook a fried breakfast. Not that I'm saying he doesn't still carry a bit of extra weight with him, but he no longer feels the need to get on a set of weighing scales for us once a week.

"It's not going to happen," I said again. Eventually, they would get the message I was sure. "Anyway, this place isn't big enough for everyone's family too."

"Well obviously we'd have it at Brian's place." Sophie rolled her eyes at me.

"And what does Brian think about that?" I looked at him sitting in the armchair with a smirk on his face. Hopefully he would read my mind. *Say no! For once in your life back me up.* I was staring at him; sure he must be able to read my thoughts by now

He flashed me his boyish smile and I knew exactly what he was thinking: *This is so much fun. I love watching them wind you up. There's no way I'm going to back you up and miss out on so much entertainment! I love you though.* Gosh, he could be annoying. But the 'I love you' look still got me every time.

"I think it sounds like fun!" Brian said.

"It's not a proper fat club if we're at Brian's though," I argued. "If we can't do it properly, like we've always done it, then surely we may as well just cancel." Since, they refused to relocate fat club, I'd at least use that to my advantage.

"But fat club is about the people, not the place." Linda's gentle voice suddenly made me want to throttle her. "Plus, we did meet at the hotel to begin with so we have changed venue before. It's certainly not unprecedented."

"She's right," Sophie agreed. "Anyway last week you spent the whole evening telling us we can't meet at Grace's house now that you're living with Brian. I think you even used the word trespassing, didn't you?"

"You really do need to give me the keys back." I glared at her and then turned on the others. "All of you! I know you all have keys." They looked at me innocently. I swear they enjoyed trying to make me look like a crazy person.

"Fine! You can have the keys back," Sophie said, finally relenting. "I can't wait for Christmas at Brian's house!" She clapped her hands together excitedly. That girl really knew how to push my buttons. I took a deep breath but I couldn't take it anymore.

"Sophie," I said through gritted teeth. "Could you please sit somewhere else?"

She pouted, clearly enjoying the fact that I was finally walking into her trap. "Why can't I sit here?" She wiggled her toes in Brian's lap and moved her perfect nineteen-year-old form closer into him. Brian had his cheeky lopsided smile and was avoiding eye contact with me.

"Just get off my boyfriend!" I exploded, giving up on trying to keep my cool.

"It's fiancé actually," Brian corrected me.

"Yes I know. But that still sounds weird." It'd taken long enough to get used to calling him my boyfriend; I still wasn't used to fiancé. "Anyway, Sophie, get off!"

"Is it because you're a crazy, jealous girlfriend?" she asked. "Because you definitely told me that you're not the jealous type."

Sometimes I think she spends whole days just thinking up ways to annoy me.

"I didn't say that to set you a challenge! I was just chatting to you about my relationship because you were doing that thing where you pretend to be a really nice, normal friend so I tell you about my life. I didn't know you were going to attempt to prove me wrong for your own entertainment."

"You should really know me better by now. So are you going to admit you're a tiny bit jealous?"

"I'm going to count to three, Sophie, and then you need to be somewhere else."

"Oooooh!" she sang.

I stood up. "One …"

She laughed and planted a big kiss on Brian's cheek.

"Two!"

Jumping up, she settled herself on the couch between Linda and Jake.

"Anyway, it's my house now too," I said as I took her place on the arm of the chair.

"What do you mean?" Sophie asked.

"You said you can't wait for Christmas at *Brian's* place, but it's actually my place now as well."

"Sorry." She looked genuinely apologetic. "So I

should've said I can't wait for Christmas at Brian and Marie's house?"

"Exactly," I said.

The three of them let out a triumphant cheer.

Brian laughed. "You walked right into that one."

"Of course, we'll be expecting turkey and all the trimmings," Jake said. "It is Christmas after all!"

I hung my head in defeat before a smile spread over my face. I'm not sure why I ever bothered to argue with them.

So much for a quiet Christmas.

Chapter 8

It turned bitterly cold in the middle of December. Anne and I kept the heating on full blast at work. The boss, Greg, would occasionally grumble that we had the place like a sauna, but mostly he stayed hidden away in his office at the back of the shop and left us to it.

December was generally a quiet month for us. People were too busy spending their money on gifts to think about booking holidays. There were a few people who came in begging us for sunny destinations but generally the run up to Christmas was an easy time. We only had a couple of days left to work and then the shop closed for a week and we got a nice break.

"How are the Christmas plans coming?" Anne asked.

"It's a nightmare," I said. "You wouldn't believe it. Everyone has special requests for food, and they want to include their own traditions. Plus, they all want to arrive at different times. And I'm supposed to keep everyone happy somehow. It feels like Mission Impossible."

"It'll be lovely, though, having such a big group of you all together."

"I guess so." I scanned through my emails,

deciding which to reply to first. "Mum's even bringing one of the dogs she looks after. The owners are taking advantage of her. I'm not sure when they actually have the dog. It practically lives at Mum's now and they just occasionally come and take it for a walk. Not that Mum minds."

Mum was so excited about Christmas. She'd been pretty hyper about it anyway, but when she heard we'd have a houseful, she was over the moon. She was surprisingly sociable. The trouble was most people found her a bit much to take. I could understand that, seeing as I tended to feel the same myself.

Anne smiled as she tapped away at her computer. I clicked reply on an email querying a cruise. My fingers were poised over the keyboard but I struggled to focus. Instead, I swivelled my chair to face Anne.

"Linda wants us all to go to a carol service at her church on Christmas Eve. Everyone agreed to it in the end, although Sophie's worried they'll ask her to confess her sins and she'll be stuck there for a week."

"It'll get you in the Christmas spirit," Anne said, echoing Linda's sentiment. She turned back to her computer, then paused and reached for her bag. "I've got something for you." She pulled a bridal magazine out of her bag and my whole body felt suddenly heavy.

"Thanks." I forced a weak smile. Anne spent far too many working hours talking about my wedding plans. She'd been so excited when Brian and I got engaged. Since then all she wanted to talk about was the wedding.

"I folded down some pages for you." She passed

me the magazine and then walked to the coffee machine at the back of the shop.

She returned to perch on the far side of my desk while I idly flipped through the pages. Suddenly Anne stuck her hand out, pointing out a wedding dress she thought would suit me.

"It's lovely." My eyes went wide at the price.

"Have you thought anymore about a date?"

"No. I need to talk it through with Brian some more."

"Weddings take a lot of planning, Marie. You really ought to set a date and then you can start booking everything and getting organised. Did you say you wanted a band at the reception?"

"No, I don't think so."

"But you will get married in church, won't you?"

"Maybe," I said. "I don't know."

"Marie! I want to shake you. Can't you be a little bit enthusiastic? It is your wedding we're talking about after all."

"It could be yours, the amount you go on about it." I spoke absentmindedly and realised my mistake when Anne fell silent. One day I'd learn to think before I spoke and be better off for it. Anne shook her head sadly. She rested her hand on mine as she finally broke the silence.

"What's wrong, Marie?"

"Nothing. What do you mean?"

"Have you got cold feet? If you don't want to get married, you need to say something. Don't string Brian along. It's not fair."

"Anne!" I snatched my hand away from hers. "Of course I want to marry Brian. I haven't got cold feet."

"Do you think I don't notice how you never want to talk about the wedding? You might not like to admit it but I know you very well. I can tell when something is bothering you. Deny it if you want, but just remember I'm here for you whenever you decide you want to talk about it."

She put her hands up in mock surrender as she moved away. I hated it when she was like this. She would now wave away any argument I made and just smile at me condescendingly.

"There's nothing to talk about," I said. She gave me the inevitable patronising smile. "Seriously. I don't have a problem. I'm going to marry Brian and live happily ever after." I don't know why I was being so defensive and why I felt like I was trying to convince myself as much as her. I loved Brian. There wasn't much not to love about him; he was pretty close to perfect. "I'm just too busy thinking about Christmas to worry about a wedding." I don't think she believed my excuse but she took the hint and changed the subject.

"Christmas isn't so difficult. Just make a list and be organised." She paused. "Okay, maybe it will be difficult for you …"

"Thanks for the support!" She was right though; I wasn't the most organised of people.

"I'll make you a list." Anne beamed at me and started scribbling away.

"I'm not sure you should be doing that on company time, Anne." I flashed a mischievous grin. She was usually the conscientious one.

"Oh shush! It's nearly Christmas. We're allowed to slack off a bit, aren't we?"

"I can't remember the exact policy. Hang on while I call Head Office and check …" I picked up the phone and then laughed as Anne directed a piece of balled up paper at my head.

I threw it back at her. "And now we're wasting paper, are we?"

"You're in a funny mood today," she said. "All the excitement of Christmas is finally getting to you, I suppose?"

"I guess I am quite excited about it now. I've never had a big Christmas before. It was always just Mum, Aunt Kath and me. It's a lot of pressure having the whole gang around, though. Everyone wants things done in a certain way otherwise it's not a proper Christmas for them."

I thought back to the previous fat club evening. Everyone had told me in great detail exactly what they were expecting on Christmas Day. When Jake had started a discussion about real gravy versus instant, I placated them all by asking them to write down any special requests they had. I'd smiled pleasantly and was surprised that they actually seemed to believe I would cater to their every whim.

Come Christmas Day I planned on getting them all drunk enough that they wouldn't care about the gravy, or which method I used to cook the turkey, or if the bloody crackers were of the luxury variety.

Anne looked at me guiltily. "Maybe I should keep the list basic?"

"Anne!" I glanced at the piece of paper as she continued to scribble away. "It looks more like an essay than a list. I don't want to see it. It'll only scare me when I realise how much I've got to do. Thank goodness we agreed to do Secret Santa so I don't have to buy gifts for everyone."

"Oh, that'll be fun. Who do you have to buy for?"

"Linda, so that's fairly simple. She's easy to please. I'll probably get a bit of something for Callum too." Jake's ten-year-old nephew, Callum, had become one of my favourite people in the world. He sometimes ended up staying at our place after a games' evening and he could always make me smile. He was just fun to be around. His mum was unreliable, so he didn't always have an easy time of it. His dad wasn't on the scene either so it was lucky he had Jake to be a stable influence in his life.

As the afternoon drew on, I caught myself involuntarily glancing at the door every few minutes and was filled with a sense of foreboding. At five o'clock on the dot, the door swung open and in ran Jason. He didn't stop; just continued running on the spot. He was like a machine.

"How's my favourite travel agent?" He winked at Anne and she beamed back at him.

Then he turned to me.

"Come on, Marie! Fitness waits for no one. Throw some lycra on and let's go burn some fat!"

Without a word, I walked past him and into the toilet to change into my jogging gear. I liked to think that as soon as I was out of sight, Jason would collapse on the floor gasping for breath. No one could actually be that fit. I'd never seen him break a sweat or get out of breath. Maybe it was a finely honed act to make him look like the best personal trainer in the world.

As always, I glanced wistfully at the tiny window

in the toilet. It hadn't magically grown and I hadn't shrunk. I definitely still had no escape route. Shoving my work clothes into my backpack, I walked out into the shop. We'd been doing the sessions for a few weeks now. There was a slight chance my fitness was improving but it was slow going.

Jason was still dancing around. For someone so big, he was extremely graceful and light on his feet. He was slightly effeminate and I always thought that if the personal training didn't work out he'd make a great drag queen.

I looked at Anne and resisted the urge to cry and cling to her like a small child.

"Come on then. Let's get it over with." I opened the shop door and took off up the road with Jason close behind.

Chapter 9

"Marie! How many times do I have to remind you about the importance of a proper warm up?" Jason overtook me effortlessly and ran backwards for a while as he talked to me.

"A few more, I guess." My lungs began to burn and my legs felt heavy. Why did I put myself through this? "If I'm not warm by the time we get to the park, I'll warm up then. But there's no way I'm stretching in the middle of town. I've told you this before. We have to get away from civilisation as quickly as possible." I focused on my breathing, unable to talk anymore.

With my head down, I ran on with no more argument from Jason. He knew better by now. There was no stopping me until I was under the cover of trees, and away from other human beings. He'd also learned not to talk to me while we ran; I'd be incapable of speech for a good while. That was my target though. If I could jog and talk at the same time, I'd have unlocked my ultimate fitness goal. I tried it last session, but only managed a raspy, "I hate you."

Once we reached the park, I collapsed onto my regular bench. After gulping down some water, I got up and followed Jason to the grass. He laid out mats for us and led me through a variety of exercises designed to torment and torture me.

We seemed to have fallen into a fairly acceptable rhythm for my workout. Jason had learned to keep talking to a minimum and to avoid any sort of encouragement. Somehow no matter whether he barked orders at me or gently asked for one more push-up, it just made me want to punch him. After shouting at him a couple of times, he'd learned that I would only do as much as I wanted and not one sit-up more. In return I was respectful enough of Jason's trade to put in as much effort as I could muster.

"You must get loads of women?" The filter between my thoughts and my mouth cut out as I lay next to Jason on the grass for my five-minute rest before the run home. It was probably going to be less than five-minutes today. It was freezing and I was looking forward to my lovely warm house.

His blue eyes twinkled when he looked at me. "Why are you always so fascinated by my love life?"

"I'm not really," I said. "But objectively speaking, you are pretty easy on the eye. And since you're young, free and single, I guess you have a lot of fun in your spare time?"

He sat up, pulling the sweatband off his head to run a hand through his silky blonde hair. "I'd say I have my fair share of fun."

I looked pointedly at his sweatband. "Those things should never have left the eighties."

He fired it at my head with a laugh. Then he jumped up and tugged my mat out from under me, indicating the end of my rest period. I hauled myself up and flicked the sweatband back at him before taking off at a sprint.

"Catch me if you can!" I called over my shoulder.

He was effortlessly striding along beside me after about three seconds.

"Are you even human?" I asked before falling into a silence which was necessary for me to make it up the hill and home.

"It still amazes me that you live in a place like this," Jason said when I handed him a glass of water in the kitchen.

"Don't get too familiar, Jason. Just remember I'm paying you for your time."

"Technically, I'm off the clock now," he said with a cheeky grin.

"You better get out then, I don't really want to be spending my time with a fitness freak for no good reason."

I enjoyed the relaxed banter with Jason and liked his easy-going nature. He usually came into the house after our run to grab a drink of water and spend a few minutes chatting before heading on to his next client.

"It really is an amazing house though." His eyes darted around the place while he moved down the hallway and towards the front door.

"I know." I smiled at him before my face fell at the sound of keys in the lock at the front door.

"Brian's home early," I whispered. Without thinking, I grabbed Jason's elbow and pulled him back toward the kitchen. "You'll have to go out of the back and down the side of the house."

"I hate being your dirty little secret. It's so sordid!" Jason chuckled when I opened the back door and shoved him through it. "Can't I stay and meet him?"

"No!" I hissed, closing the door quietly behind him.

"Hi!" Brian's voice drifted in from the hallway. I grabbed my backpack and tiptoed up the stairs.

"Hi!" I called back once I was safely upstairs. "I'm just getting changed. You're early."

"Yeah, I've been working too hard. I said I had a migraine and ducked out early. Do you want to go out for dinner?"

"Sounds good," I shouted as I peeled off my sweaty clothes and shoved them into the washing basket. "I'm going to jump in the shower. I'll be down in five minutes."

The one good thing about my workout with Jason was that I could now go out and stuff myself without feeling guilty.

Brian was sitting on a stool in the kitchen when I came downstairs. I gave him a quick kiss. "Where do you want to eat?"

"Actually, do you mind if we stay in? Now I've sat down I've lost motivation."

"Fine by me." I moved over to the sink to get another glass of water and noticed Jason's water glass sitting next to mine by the sink. I looked at Brian who was watching me intensely. "Everything okay?" I asked nervously.

He shrugged. "Fine."

I was overcome by a wave of guilt and had an urge to confess my sins of exercise and beg Brian's forgiveness. Although, realistically he'd probably just had a bad day at work. Surely he hadn't actually been upset by the fact that there were two water glasses by the sink; that would be weird even for his slightly obsessive neat-freak tendencies.

The secrecy was turning me into a nervous wreck and - with hindsight - ushering Jason out the backdoor had been a little bit dramatic. I would tell Brian soon. It was a silly thing to keep secret.

Brian looked exhausted and he rested his head on my chest when I wrapped my arms around him.

"Come on," I said. "Couch, food, and an early night. It's almost Christmas; just a couple more days and then you'll get a proper break from work. That's what you need."

He followed me into the living room and sat quietly on the couch.

"Do you want a beer?" I said.

He shook his head and took my hand to pull me down beside him. The silence was weird. "Are you really okay?" Automatically, I put a hand across his forehead as though he was a small child. No idea what I hoped to achieve.

It made him laugh at least. He pushed my hand away. "I'm fine. Just tired. Tell me about your day."

"Same as always, really." I thought for a moment, then rolled my eyes. "Anne brought me a bridal magazine into work. She'd already been through it and folded pages down of anything she thought I might like."

"That makes it easier," he said.

"Yes." I smiled. "She's a bit obsessed."

"It's nice that she takes an interest."

I nodded.

"So did she have any good ideas?"

"For the wedding?" I shrugged. "It's the usual wedding stuff; white dresses and flowers and fancy cakes."

"We should probably decide on a venue," he said. "If we want the wedding next year?"

"It probably won't be next year." I frowned. "I don't want to be in a rush to organise it and end up one of those crazy bridezillas."

"I don't think there's much chance of that." He had his arm around me and slowly stroked my arm. "I'm sure we could manage to organise it for next year. What do you think, a registry office and then the reception elsewhere, or a church ceremony …"

"I don't know."

"What about having it at a hotel?"

"I don't know."

He sat up straighter. "You must have some idea. You said you'd think about it."

"I'm still thinking."

"But you don't have any preference for a venue?"

I rubbed my eyes. "Not really. What do *you* think?"

"I'd be happy with anything," he said. "Whatever you want."

"Well, that's not helpful either, is it? You can't be annoyed with me for not having ideas, and then not have any yourself."

"Hotel, then," he said. "Somewhere out in the countryside. Everyone can stay over. We could make it a whole weekend affair."

My cheeks puffed out as I blew out a breath.

"You don't like my idea?" Brian asked.

"It sounds fine."

"You don't sound very enthusiastic. If you don't like that, suggest something else."

I stood and went to plug in the Christmas lights. "I'm not sure what the rush is to decide. I've got so much to organise for Christmas. Can you just let me get that out of the way before you make me plan a wedding?"

When I turned he was staring at me.

"Sorry," I said quickly. "But you're stressed with work. I'm stressed about Christmas. It seems like a bad time to start organising the wedding."

"I thought it'd be fun to organise. I'm not saying we have to start booking everything, but we could just start thinking about it. It'd be something to look forward to."

"You're right." I forced a tight smile. "I'll get you a beer and grab Anne's magazine. We can have a flick through. I'll see what I can whip up for dinner too."

I gave him a kiss and he seemed to be placated. Spending the evening going through bridal magazines wasn't really my idea of fun but I'd at least got the nodding and smiling down to a tee thanks to Anne.

HANNAH ELLIS

Chapter 10

It was a week before Christmas. Amazingly, Brian made it home from work at a reasonable time so we weren't rushing straight out the door for fat club. He'd come home early for a few days in a row.

After the day I'd shoved Jason out the back door, I'd decided to take a break from exercising. I told Jason I was giving it up until the New Year. It was like a Christmas gift to myself. And it worked out well since Brian had started coming home early. I didn't have to worry about explaining my foray into the world of fitness. He'd definitely tease me, and if Brian knew, it would only be a matter of time before Sophie found out. Me exercising was far too much ammunition for jokes for her.

Jason hadn't taken it well but I'd promised to get back to it with renewed vigour in January. That had earned me a lecture about how the Christmas period was the exact time I should be thinking about exercise. He'd gone on about indulging in too much junk and alcohol over the Christmas period. I told him that was exactly what I intended to do. It was Christmas after all.

"Are you okay?" I asked Brian. I'd whipped up spaghetti carbonara and we sat on the barstools at the island in the kitchen to eat. Brian was pretty quiet and only seemed to be pushing the pasta round the plate. Admittedly I wasn't the world's greatest cook, but he usually wasn't fussy when it came to food.

"Fine," he said with a weary smile. "Did you get a message from Sophie?"

"Yes." I sucked a string of spaghetti up. "I ignored it."

"Why do you think she wants us to wear black?"

"No idea." I'd decided I wasn't going to fall into the trap of asking her. "There'll be some ridiculous reason. Her goldfish died or she broke a nail or something. I ignored the message. Except, I did remind her we're meeting here from now on and not at Grace's house."

"That's not going to happen," he said.

"In January I'm putting my foot down. I'll get the locks changed at Grace's place or call the police on them or something."

"I'd actually really love to see the police officer's face when the three of them explained why they were there."

"It would be quite entertaining," I agreed. "Anyway, how was your day?"

"Boring. How was yours?"

I tilted my head to one side. "We have this same conversation everyday. You never tell me about work."

"Because it's utterly boring and I'd rather hear about your day."

"It doesn't seem very fair. I bore you with my day, I'm quite happy to listen to you tell me about yours."

"Your day's entertaining. I like hearing your stories about Anne, or how you fell off your chair."

"One time!" I laughed. "And I really wish I hadn't told you that."

"My day's all meetings and numbers. I'd bore you to death."

"One day you should try leaning back too far in your chair!"

"Did you do it just so you had a funny story for me?"

I grinned. "Of course. That's true love for you."

His smile was half-hearted as he stood and cleared the dishes away. "We better get going and see why it's black day at fat club."

When we arrived at Grace's place, Sophie, Linda and Jake were sitting on the couch. Jake was wearing a black suit, while Sophie and Linda both had black dresses on.

"What's going on?" I asked. "Are you all in mourning?"

"Yes," Sophie said wearily. "Did you not get the message?"

I ignored the question. "What are we mourning?"

"The end of an era," Jake said.

Sophie pointed at the coffee table. There was a cake on it and I leaned down to read the squiggly writing in the icing. *Goodbye Grace's house.*

I gasped. "What's happening?"

"It's our last day here," Linda said.

"Oh, I like how you decorated the cake with keys." I leaned in closer. "Wait. Are they the actual house keys." I picked one off. "That's really unhygienic."

"It's not really the time to worry about a few germs." Sophie sighed dramatically. "It's a very sad day."

"We shouldn't have cake at fat club." I perched on the arm of the chair beside Brian. "It's disrespectful to the original meetings."

Sophie laughed. "Do you remember when Linda first said that? We had that massive row?"

"You attacked Jake with the tube of Pringles," I reminded her happily. Then my shoulders sagged as I looked around the room. It really did feel like the end of an era. "I wish I'd worn black now."

"I'll never forget that first day I met you all here," Brian said. "I was standing on the doorstep and Jake and Sophie barged past me."

"That was the first day we all came here," Sophie said. "Linda turned up later, crying."

"I'm at it again now," she said, rooting in her handbag for a tissue. "I'll miss this place."

"We'll still meet up every week," Brian said cheerfully.

"No need to encourage them," I said quietly.

"It won't be the same," Jake said. "Our little group might fall apart completely."

"It's the people, not the place," I reminded them. "Isn't that what Linda said?"

"I might have been wrong," she said with a sniff.

I stood up. "How about we all eat some germ-infested cake and cheer up?"

It ended up being a fun evening. We reminisced about all the crazy times we'd spent together in Grace's living room. There were some really funny stories and we laughed a lot as we recalled them.

Between us, we polished off the cake and I wiped off the keys on a napkin.

"I can't believe you actually returned the keys. I thought I'd never convince you." My eyes darted to Sophie. "Did you get more cut and this is just you winding me up? Are you still planning on meeting here?"

"No." She laughed. "We're meeting at your place from now on."

I looked at her suspiciously. After so long trying to convince them of the change in venue, I was suspicious of the sudden turnaround.

Sophie's eyes twinkled. "This is definitely the last meeting at Grace's house." She paused. "When Brian gave us keys to your place he made us promise to give up Grace's keys."

My eyes widened as my gaze shot to Brian. "You better not have!"

He laughed loudly. "She's winding you up."

"She better be." I glared at him and then Sophie. It was always hard to tell who was winding me up on Thursday evenings.

"Are you okay?" Brian asked when we stood on the doorstep waving as Linda's car pulled away. She was generally the designated driver for the three of them on Thursdays.

"It feels weird," I said walking back into the living room and gazing around. "I feel really nostalgic."

"We had some good times here didn't we?" He parked himself on the arm of the couch.

"We had some *great* times." I sighed. "Do you remember when we got drunk and woke up to the bird in the kitchen?"

His mouthed twitched to a smile. "That was a little bit crazy." I nodded and he looked at me seriously.

"That's always what I loved about you. My life was really boring until you came along. Anytime I was with you, I never knew what might happen."

I sighed happily. "We don't really have nights like that anymore, do we?"

"Did we get boring?" he asked with an odd look on his face.

I shook my head. "I don't think so. Do you?"

"I'm happy," he said.

"Me too." I stood and took his hand to walk to the door. "And I'm sure Thursday nights at our house will be just as much fun as Thursday nights here."

It was still very odd to close the door to Grace's house and think that fat club wouldn't meet there anymore.

Chapter 11

On the Saturday before Christmas, instead of our usual shopping trip, Linda picked me up and drove me out of town, to the health spa where Sophie worked. It was our pre-Christmas treat.

"Good afternoon! Welcome to the Eden Day Spa." An overly made up woman with a fixed smile greeted us at the reception desk.

"We're looking for Sophie," I said.

Sophie appeared from a side door and waved at us frantically. "I can't believe I finally got you here! You're going to have the best time." She smiled at the woman on the reception desk and led us through the elegant foyer. Sophie was wearing a pristine white tunic and white tailored trousers. Her hair was neatly tied up in a bun and her make up was subtle but pretty. It was strange to see her at work and looking so professional. She seemed more than her nineteen years and I felt oddly proud of her.

"Don't be angry with me but I had a little mix up ..." She looked at us with a nervous smile. "I double booked and now I have this regular customer waiting for me and she won't see anyone else. But it's fine because a couple of the other girls are available and said they would do your treatments." She grinned at us and we glared at her in response.

"Oh come on. It'll be fine. You'll still have a nice time and I'll pop in whenever I get a minute, to see how you're getting on. Then we can over to the hotel later and have a drink in the bar. It's really fancy over there. You'll love it."

"Sophie!" I huffed. "You said you'd give us facials. You promised it would be you giving us treatments."

"You'll be fine. I told the girls to look after you really well."

"It won't be as much fun without you though," Linda said.

"Well, duh! Of course not!" she said. "Come on through. The girls will be waiting for you. And they're doing this as a favour so be nice to them."

Sophie opened the door and led us into a deserted room. "They're supposed to be here." She looked back at us confused. "I'm sure they'll be here any minute so just wait here. I have to go but I'll be back soon."

I shouted after her in annoyance but she ignored me and hurried away.

Frowning at Linda, I hopped into one of the fancy chairs. I relaxed back into it and felt much better about things. "If they don't come to give us the facials we can do them for each other," I said. "How hard can it be anyway?"

She took a seat in the chair next to me. A moment later the door opened and I sat up quickly. Two young girls dressed in white walked in.

Neither of them made eye contact until they were directly in front of us, at which point they bowed slightly.

The brunette in front of me had an odd look on her face. Her smile looked slightly painful and her eyes seemed too wide open. She barely blinked. "Welcome to the Eden Day Spa," she said in a slightly creepy tone. "Sit back and relax." Her incessant stare was making me nervous.

Eventually, she took a seat on a little stool on castors and rolled close to me. "First, I shall assess your skin."

I was pinned to the chair as she ran a finger along my forehead and pulled at my cheeks. She sighed a lot and I could swear she even rolled her eyes at one point. I just sat there, stunned. Sophie definitely said they would be nice. When I glanced over, Linda was also being poked and prodded, but her girl at least looked a little friendlier.

"There are some fine lines on your forehead and around your eyes," my girl said. I was slightly taken aback. I thought they were supposed to relax us, not tell me how many wrinkles I had.

"This is quite worrying at your age," she added. "You really need to take care of your skin. I can recommend a good moisturiser, which will take care of the fine lines. It's only £60 and it really is a miracle in a bottle."

I couldn't help but chuckle. "Don't they call them laughter lines? I think I'll save some money and just cut down on the laughter. I'll hang on until after Christmas, but then the laughter will stop!"

Linda's girl looked amused but mine stayed straight-faced. I tried to break her with a smile but she just ran a finger down the side of my face. "You have some redness and dry spots; your skin tone is very uneven. What cleanser do you use in your skincare routine?"

I resisted the urge to laugh loudly at the mention of my skincare routine. It crossed my mind to make something up but I didn't have the energy.

"I tend to just fall into bed at night. If I've made an effort with the make up then I might grab a make-up removing baby wipe thing and have a quick scrub at the old eyes. That's about it, though."

"Well then there's no wonder." She rolled her eyes but looked sympathetic. "Don't worry. It's never too late to start a good skincare routine. You're in luck today. We have a fantastic pack that includes the most amazing cleanser, toner and moisturiser, and it's on offer at the moment. It's 20% off so it's a steal at £200. I'll talk to you more about it later but I really can't recommend it highly enough."

I glanced at Linda who looked as shocked as I was. Presumably, when she referred to it as a steal, she meant that they'd be robbing me blind.

"I'll just need to see the diamond-encrusted, solid gold box - which I assume it comes in - before I decide."

Linda grinned at me but the brunette ignored me and continued with her sales pitch. "You'll need a decent exfoliator as well to tackle those blackheads – you can see those from across the room."

She smiled then. The cheek of her. "Now, lie back and relax. Let's take a few minutes to soothe those tired eyes." She wheeled over and took a cold facemask from a fridge and then placed it over my eyes. "I'm going to dim the lights and you can take a few minutes to listen to the calming sounds." She switched on a CD and ocean sounds filled the room.

"Now, as we leave you for a few moments, just focus on your breathing and feel your body relax." She was using the hushed creepy tones again.

"I think I'm going to struggle to relax now," I said. "I'm too busy worrying about my terrible, uneven skin and all my wrinkles."

"Don't forget all those blackheads," Linda said. I had to lift my eye mask to look at her. It wasn't very often that Linda cracked a joke.

"Exactly, Linda! How could I possibly relax?" Linda's girl was stifling laughter while mine was still managing to look serious.

"And relax ..." She hushed me.

When they left the room, I raised the mask to look at Linda again. "I'm going to kill Sophie!"

She lifted one side of her eye mask and smiled at me. "It's not so bad. This eye thing is nice."

"It's not so bad for you with your lovely skin! Your girl's nice too. Why did I get stuck with dragon lady? I'm not sure how she got a job here. She's horrible."

"I feel a bit sorry for her actually." Linda lowered her eye mask again. "She's not got it easy today; trying to sort out your skin!"

"Linda! What's got into you? You're a laugh a minute!"

She smiled smugly and I lay back and tried to relax.

"Marie!" Sophie hissed next to me, making me jump.

I peered out at her. "What are you doing sneaking around?"

"What did you do?" she demanded.

"What do you mean?"

"Jill is out there in tears. She said you keep mocking her when she's trying to give you advice …"

"Hey! She shouldn't go around trying to diminish people's self-confidence. You should have heard the things she was saying about my skin. I was only trying to lighten the atmosphere. It was a case of make jokes or cry."

"Well you've made *her* cry. She's really upset. She's only trying to help. You should listen to her. She really knows what she's doing."

"Fine. I'll be nice."

The door opened then and the girls in white returned. "Marie was just saying how sorry she is. Weren't you, Marie?" Sophie gave me a nudge.

"Yes. I'm sorry." I forced the words out and felt like a child. Sophie nudged me again so I elaborated. "I'm just having a hard time, what with my terrible skin and everything! The jokes are just a defence mechanism. Don't take it personally."

She nodded her acceptance and Sophie headed back out of the room.

"Just relax …" Jill pulled the eye mask firmly back over my eyes. I lay there for a minute, feeling slightly awkward and wondering what was coming next. I finally peeked out from my eye mask and saw the girls huddled over a sink at the other side of the room. The lights were dim but I could've sworn they were tussling over a bottle of vodka. I knew they were doing the treatment as a favour to Sophie but surely they should still take it a bit seriously. They jumped as I cleared my throat loudly.

"And now we will get started on the exfoliation," the blonde girl said in the creepy hushed tones.

Jill tried to discreetly put the bottle back under the sink while I strained to see if it really was vodka. She moved to the next cupboard and looked up at the blonde. "I'm not sure what to use?"

"Try the brush," the blonde girl said, pointing.

Jill pulled out what looked to be a shoe brush and I cringed. "I don't think that will do it though. I might try this …" Jill spoke as if I wasn't in the room and pulled a large loofah out of the cupboard. Surely she wasn't thinking of coming near my face with that. I started to panic slightly as she turned and moved towards me. Flinging the eye mask to one side, I jumped out of the chair.

"Stop!" I shouted.

"What's wrong?" She looked far too innocent for someone wielding a loofah and intending to scrape my face off with it. "It's for those nasty dry bits. You'll be amazed at the difference, I promise." She smiled sweetly and I backed into a wall unit.

The door swung open and Sophie walked in, looking at me like I was insane. "What are you doing?"

I pointed at Jill. "She wants to ruin my face!"

Sophie narrowed her eyes and shook her head. "It's to exfoliate your dry skin, that's all. Just sit down and stop embarrassing me, will you?"

"But … but …" there was no way I was going to let her near my face with that instrument of torture. "She's drunk!"

"Marie!" Sophie shouted at me. "What's wrong with you?"

"She is. I saw them drinking." I sidestepped towards the sink to retrieve the evidence. Everyone was looking at me as though I'd lost the plot. "Look!" I waved the bottle of vodka at them victoriously.

"Sorry." Jill looked at Sophie. "I accidentally kicked her bag and that rolled out. I didn't want to say anything because she's your friend but I couldn't have her sneaking a drink every time we left the room. She already seemed a bit unstable to start with."

"What?!" I screeched, unable to take in what was going on around me. "We just came for a bit of pampering and now I have no idea what's going on."

"Is that because you're drunk?" Sophie asked me calmly. "Do you really think I haven't noticed you behaving strangely lately? I've been a bit worried about you. We all have." She looked over at Linda who was nervously looking at the floor. "Just put the vodka down, please." Sophie moved towards me as though she was approaching a ticking bomb.

I looked at the bottle of vodka and then placed it down next to the sink. "Why on earth would you be worried about me?"

Linda looked up at me. "You've been so … what's the word? Happy … and smiley."

"It's all the smiling that's really had us worried," Sophie added.

"Yes." Linda nodded. "And the laughing too. There's been a lot of laughing."

The corners of Sophie's mouth started to twitch and Linda broke into a grin. The two girls in white were stifling giggles too. I relaxed and felt the laughter bubbling up as I realised what was going on.

"Sophie! Was this all a big joke?"

She burst out laughing and started to back away from me.

"I'm going to kill you!" I moved towards her and broke into a run as she hurried to get away from me. I chased her around the room a couple of times before stopping in front of Jill. "You!" I pointed an accusing finger at her. "You're so mean."

"I'm so sorry!" She attempted to quell the laughter. "Sophie said she'd buy us drinks if we played a joke on you. I'm sorry. It was fun though. The blackheads!"

I looked at Linda. "Were you in on this?"

"Well, it was just a bit of fun!"

"I had to tell Linda," Sophie said. "I was worried she'd get upset if she thought it was real."

"But you've no regard for my feelings? I'm going to need professional help to build up my self-confidence again. My poor skin!"

"You needed bringing down a bit anyway," Sophie said. "You think you're God's gift to men since you landed yourself a hot boyfriend!" I grabbed the loofah from Jill and threw it at Sophie's head before moving to the sink to retrieve the bottle of vodka.

"I've earned this," I said as I removed the top. I felt fairly sheepish as I took a long swig of lukearm water.

HANNAH ELLIS

Chapter 12

I admired my newly manicured nails while I sat in the hotel bar with Sophie and Linda an hour later.

"I told you you'd enjoy a bit of pampering," Sophie said.

I smiled at her. It had been really lovely. Jill and her blonde friend, Beth, had given Linda and me facials and manicures while Sophie sat and chatted to us. We were all in a bit of a silly mood after Sophie's prank and the atmosphere was light and fun.

"What do you think of this place then?" Sophie asked, looking around the fancy hotel. We were sitting at a table next to the bar sipping exotic looking cocktails.

"Very fancy," I said.

"I was thinking you could get married here. There's a little lake with a boathouse out the back. It's gorgeous in the summer. They do these weekend packages. You get pampered in the spa and have the ceremony in the boathouse and then you can either have a marquee on the lawn for the reception or have it inside here. We could all stay in the hotel for the weekend."

"That sounds wonderful," Linda agreed.

I took a long sip of my cocktail and tried to keep calm. "Have you been talking to Brian? He was talking about doing something similar."

"Great minds think alike," Sophie said. "So what do you think?"

I scanned the room and curled my lip. "Maybe."

"Well, you're full of enthusiasm!" Sophie rolled her eyes. "I have these great ideas and all you can manage is a maybe? If Brian thinks it's a good idea too, why not?"

"I feel like Brian only suggested getting married in a hotel because he thinks it's the sort of thing I'd want. I'm not sure he really wants that."

"Who cares what Brian wants? It's your big day."

"His too."

"Let's be honest, it's all about the bride. Plus, Brian will agree to anything you want. He's well trained."

"I'm just not sure what I want yet," I said. "I don't think I want a big do."

"You've got loads of time to decide," Linda said kindly. "You only get one wedding so you should make sure you do what you want. A wedding by the lake would be lovely though, wouldn't it? Sitting out under the stars in the evening and sipping champagne."

"Sounds nice," I agreed.

"I wish you'd set a date so I can get properly excited," Sophie said. "How many bridesmaids will you have?"

I looked at her to see how long she could pull off the innocent look under scrutiny. She shifted in her seat and looked uncomfortable. I saw a flash of vulnerability that was rare in Sophie. It was tempting to tell her she could be my bridesmaid, just to see her face light up. I'd hesitated too long, though, and couldn't bring myself to do it.

"I'm not even sure I want bridesmaids. We'll probably just do something really quiet." Neither of them managed to hide their disappointment and it annoyed me slightly. I wished people would just stop asking about the wedding. Couldn't they leave me to decide in my own time?

"Anyway, I don't know what to get Brian for Christmas," I said in a bid to change the subject.

"You're leaving it a bit late," Linda said.

I raised my eyebrows. "Not helpful!"

"We do some nice products for men," Sophie said. "I can swipe you some samples if you want?"

"I was thinking of something a bit more meaningful ..."

"How about a watch?" Linda suggested.

"I think he's got about three already."

"That's the trouble, isn't it?" Sophie said. "What do you get for the man who has everything? Maybe make a voucher for something. Like a night of passion but something you wouldn't normally do ... a threesome maybe?"

"Sophie!"

"I'm just trying to help!"

"That's not helping."

"Okay then, let me think. What about a weekend away?"

"I considered it but I want to get something I can wrap up. It's a bit boring isn't it, just telling him that we'll go away sometime in the near future. I want to get him something really fun. He's been in a bit of a strange mood recently and I feel like he needs cheering up."

"That's not like Brian," Linda said.

"I think it's work stress. He's been coming home early the last week so at least he's trying to take it a bit easier. He's got some time off now so hopefully he'll relax and get back to his usual self."

"I'm sure a break will do him good," Linda said.

"Fingers crossed. Anyway, what can I buy him that's fun? Sophie, you have loads of boys to buy for, what do you get them?"

She shook her head. "You mean my brothers? I'm buying them Nerf guns but they're children."

"That's not a bad idea," I mused.

Sophie laughed. "Don't buy Brian a Nerf gun. He'll think you've gone crazy!"

"What's a Nerf gun?" Linda asked.

"It's a toy gun that shoots foam pellets," Sophie said. "And it's a toy. For little boys!"

"I think it's a good idea," I said with a grin.

"Well then maybe we should take this away from you …" Sophie playfully reached for my cocktail.

Linda smiled at me. "You know, I think deep down all men are just little boys!"

Chapter 13

I'd been a little sceptical about the spa day but it turned out to be a really good fun. I was still laughing about Sophie's prank when I got home.

Unfortunately, I was enveloped by Brian's bad mood pretty much as soon as I walked in the door. He sat at the dining table hunched over his laptop. When I put my hand on his neck, he flinched. I wasn't sure if he jumped because he'd only just noticed me or because he objected to my touch. The tension radiated from him.

"Everything okay?" I asked.

"Fine." He stretched his neck and brushed my hand aside at the same time.

"I thought you were all finished with work until after Christmas."

"No." He sounded annoyed, as though I was asking stupid questions. "I've got a lot of work to do."

"But you said you weren't going into the office again between now and Christmas."

He kept his eyes firmly on his laptop. "I'm not going into the office. I'm sick of the place. I'll work from home though."

"Okay." I pulled out the chair beside him. "Are you nearly finished? I was thinking we could get dinner in town and go ice-skating. The Ice rink's all set up beside the Christmas market. It looks so pretty all lit up. It's lovely and festive. A break would probably do you good."

"I've got loads of work to do," he said. There was a hint of irritation to his voice, like he'd rather I left him alone.

"It was fun with Sophie and Linda today." I wasn't sure he was even listening to me as he went back to tapping on his laptop. I kept talking anyway. "She played this stupid joke on me where she pretended she had another client and got her friends to–"

"I'm really busy." Brian's shoulders tensed and he clenched his jaw. "I'm never going to get to bed at this rate."

"Sorry." I stood quickly, surprised by his tone. "I'll leave you to it. What do you fancy for dinner?" I had my hand on his shoulder but he squirmed away from me.

"I don't care," he muttered. "I'm not hungry."

"Sorry." I backed out of the room and had no control over the tears that stung my eyes. My stomach felt as though it had twisted into a tight knot. I'd never seen Brian like that. In the living room, I lowered myself onto the couch feeling like I'd been punched in the gut. What on earth just happened?

It was about ten minutes later when I heard Brian come in the living room. He hovered in the doorway for a minute and I could tell he'd calmed down and had come to apologise.

"I'm sorry," he whispered as he walked over and sat beside me. He took my hand. "I'm really sorry."

I tried to keep calm but I was fighting off tears and feeling stupid. It seemed ridiculous to be so upset just because he was in a bad mood. It was so unlike him though. He wrapped his arms around me, and apologised again.

"It's fine." It wasn't really; I was angry with him. At the same time, his arms around me were comforting. I clung to him when he hugged me.

Finally, I took a breath and pulled away from him. "What's going on with you?"

"I'm sorry." He squeezed his eyes tight shut and then buried his head in his hands. "I'm so stressed. I shouldn't take it out on you though."

"No job is worth this," I said, stroking the hair at the back of his neck. "Tell them you're ill and you'll be off until after Christmas. Or January even. You need a break."

"It's not that easy."

I pulled him to face me. "I need you to take a break. I don't want to walk around my own home wondering if you'll bite my head off for asking what you want for dinner."

"I'm sorry."

"I know! Don't keep apologising. Just take a break. You need to relax."

He nodded gravely.

"I'll see what there is for dinner." I left him and I headed for the kitchen.

"Let's go out," Brian said, joining me in the kitchen as I peered into the fridge.

"I don't really feel like it now."

"Please." He came and snaked his arms around my waist. "Let's go ice skating."

"You didn't want to."

"I did. I was just too caught up in work. You're

right; I need to take some time off." His eyebrows knitted together. "I really want to go ice skating with you."

"No you don't." I relaxed in his arms.

He chuckled. "Okay, I'll rephrase: I will happily go ice-skating with you. And I'd really like you to agree because I feel guilty about being so grumpy and horrible."

"In that case I will go ice-skating with you."

"Thank you." He kissed my cheek and I felt better immediately. I just hoped he really would take a break from work.

We got a taxi into town. I used to take taxis all the time due to my aversion to buses and inability to drive, but it had become a much rarer occurrence since I got together with Brian. He drove me around a lot. He'd even been trying to convince me to learn to drive but I wasn't quite convinced that would ever happen.

There was a local taxi firm that I always used and I knew all the drivers well. It was always lovely to catch up with them. Unfortunately Pat drove us into town. He was my least favourite driver and not at all chatty.

Instead, I sat in the back with Brian and filled him in on my day with Linda and Sophie. He seemed to relax a little but he still wasn't quite his usual self. Even though he was trying to be very attentive, he was clearly distracted.

It was lovely at the Christmas market. I held Brian's hand and dragged him around all the little stalls. We ate German sausages and had a glass of mulled wine to warm us up. Then we wandered over to the ice rink.

"We can just watch," I said, leaning against Brian. "We don't have to skate."

"I thought you wanted to?"

"In theory, yes. It seems very romantic. But I'll probably spend most my time on my bum. Or I'll break an arm or something. That would be just my luck right before Christmas." I put my head on his shoulder. "I'm happy just watching."

We stood for a few minutes, watching people of varying skill levels glide around the ice.

"Come on," Brian finally said. "Let's give it a go."

"I honestly think I'll probably break a limb." Reluctantly, I followed him to the skate hire booth and told the guy my shoe size.

"They're not the most comfy things," I said as we sat side-by-side lacing them up. "This is going to be really embarrassing. When we were watching, I was only really waiting for people to fall. That's the only reason people watch."

"At least we might keep the crowd entertained then."

"I'm a bit scared." I struggled to even walk over to the ice in the skates.

"Shall I get you one of those penguins that the kids use to hold on to?" Brian grinned at me and stepped onto the ice.

"You actually might have to," I said.

"You can hold me instead."

I took his hand when he reached out to me.

"I'm going to fall," I said in a panic.

"No, you're not," Brian said gently. "Just keep

hold of me. And stop looking at your feet."

"Okay." I looked up at Brian and frowned. "You're skating backwards."

He nodded and pushed off a little so we moved a bit faster. I clung to both his hands.

"You can skate?" I asked.

"I was a child prodigy figure skater," he said.

My eyes widened. "Really?"

"No." He laughed. "I played ice hockey when I was a kid."

I tried to playfully slap him, but lost my balance and he had to grab hold of me to stop me from falling. "I actually believed you!"

"How can you be that gullible?"

"I'm just very trusting. And you're a very good liar. Plus, I could definitely imagine you as a figure skater!"

He laughed and moved beside me. I kept a tight hold of his arm as I shuffled around the ice. After a couple of laps, I loosened up and felt a bit more confident. Brian let go of me for a minute and skated around me a few times.

"Show off," I said, reaching for his hand again. "I can't believe you can ice skate. You're so bloody perfect. It can be a bit annoying sometimes you know."

"I'm sorry. Would you rather I was falling on my bum every five minutes?"

"Yes! I would be highly entertained."

He came to a stop in the middle of the ice rink and wrapped his arms around my waist.

I snaked my arms up around his neck. "Should we get ambitious and try a few dancing on ice moves?"

"I thought you wanted to avoid broken limbs?"

"I'm getting good though, aren't I?"

"You're a natural."

"And you're a natural liar!"

He leaned down and planted a kiss on my freezing cold nose. "I love you."

"I love you too," I said.

"Despite me being annoyingly perfect?"

"I see beyond the perfections!"

His smile slipped slightly. "Sorry for snapping at you earlier."

"It's fine. Let's just forget about it."

"You know I couldn't live without you."

I bit my lip, wondering why he was being so serious and sentimental. "You won't have to. I don't think. I'm not dying, am I?"

He laughed again. "No. I was just saying."

I kissed his lips and then pressed lightly on his chest.

"What are you doing?" he asked.

"Trying to make you wobble. How can you be as sturdy on ice as you are on solid ground?"

"Dig a toe in the ice. It's easy."

I looked down at my skates and lost my balance. My legs did a little Bambi routine under me and I grabbed at Brian. He saved me from falling yet again.

When I regained my balance, I cracked up laughing. "Are you sure we couldn't dance on the ice?!" I said mockingly. "I think I'm really graceful."

He lifted my arm above my head and twirled me carefully under it. I cheered when I didn't fall over, then kissed him again.

"Let's go home," I said.

It felt like I was pushing my luck staying on the ice much longer. I should get off while I was still in one piece.

Ice-skating had at least loosened Brian up a bit. It had freaked me out to see him in such a bad mood. Thank goodness Christmas was only a few days away. He'd definitely unwind then.

Chapter 14

It was early evening when Brian and I arrived at Linda's church on Christmas Eve.

"It's not an outdoor event, is it?" I was slightly puzzled by the number of people hanging around the spacious churchyard. It was freezing cold. Why weren't they going inside? "Oh, it is, isn't it? You'd think Linda would have mentioned that. I'd have worn more layers if I'd known. I might actually freeze to death."

"I'll keep you warm," Brian said, slinging an arm around me.

"I said we'd meet everyone outside, but it's going to be difficult to find them now."

"There's Sophie." Brian veered me off the path in her direction.

"Get off the headstone!" I said in lieu of a greeting. I pulled her off the grave and back towards the main path and the crowd of people by the church.

"No one told me it was an outdoor event," Sophie complained. "I thought I'd at least have a hard pew to snooze on."

I was disappointed too but didn't comment. There wasn't much we could do about it now. We could hardly sneak away.

"Where's Jeff?" I asked. "Is he coming?"

I wasn't quite sure what was going on with Sophie and Jeff. They'd seemed really happy for a while but things didn't seem to be going so well in recent weeks. I hadn't had a chance to quiz her about it properly.

"I don't know. He was supposed to meet me at my mum's house but I got fed up of waiting for him. I guess he got held up at work."

"Can't you call him?"

She shrugged. "He'll turn up."

"There you are." Jake hurried over to us with his partner Michael and nephew Callum close behind. "I thought we were late."

"Yoo-hoo! Everyone!" We turned to see Linda waving at us, possibly the most animated I've ever seen her.

"This is our lovely vicar!" She gestured the man beside her. He was greeted by a variety of hello's, waves and nods. Then Sophie stepped forward and curtsied, crossed herself and finally saluted him for good measure.

"Sorry!" she said. "I wasn't quite sure what to go with."

Linda looked suitably mortified.

"I think you covered most bases," the vicar replied, amused. "But I tend to just go for a handshake. You must be Sophie? I've heard a lot about you all." He offered her his hand to shake. "I'm Ted."

Sophie's eyes lit up. "No? You can't be serious? You're Father Ted?! Brilliant!" She laughed while the rest of us exchanged glances and tried to keep straight faces.

He looked thoroughly entertained by Sophie.

"Unfortunately I'm not Catholic, so we don't use Father, but I have been tempted to convert just so I could introduce myself as Father Ted. I do a good Irish accent too."

"Can I call you Father Ted anyway? It'll be our little joke. Go on, it is Christmas!"

He laughed. "I suppose so."

Sophie clapped her hands together, delighted. Then she turned to me and attempted an Irish accent. "Marie, have ye met Father Ted here? Father Ted this is Marie, sure it is. Would ye come and say hello?" She fell about laughing and the rest of us joined in.

Callum crept up next to her and gave her a friendly shove. "You're such an idiot."

"You must be Callum?" Ted said cheerfully. "It's lovely to put some faces to the names. Right, I need to get on and get the proceedings started. I want to be out of here in time for a couple of drinks in the pub." He smiled at us and then caught himself. "I mean, I need to go and spread the good word about Jesus to those who can't come here to hear it. Field work is how I think of it." He gave us a wink and headed back toward the small crowd.

Jeff arrived looking out of breath and annoyed. "You could've waited for me," he said, glaring at Sophie. "I must've just missed you, and then your mum roped me into taking the kids to the park for a run around." Sophie's younger brothers adored her boyfriend, Jeff, and it seemed like her mum took every opportunity to take advantage of that.

"I didn't want to sit around waiting for you all day!" Sophie snapped at him. "And why don't you just say no to my mum? She shouldn't be getting you to take the kids out."

"I was just trying to be helpful. Anyway, I like spending time with them." Jeff looked around our little group. "Hi everyone! Sorry I'm late."

"Don't worry," Linda said. "It's only just starting. Come on."

"Trouble in paradise?" Brian asked me quietly as we made our way across the churchyard.

"Seems like it," I replied, linking my arm through his and snuggling close enough to feel his body heat. "I feel sorry for Jeff. He's a lovely guy. Sophie walks all over him."

"It's Sophie. What do you expect?"

"Yeah, I know. She'd walk all over anyone, but she seems really disinterested all of a sudden."

"Maybe you should talk to her."

"I think I'm probably better off staying out of it."

We slowed as we got to the entrance of the church and joined the huddle of people looking up at the choir who were standing on the front steps.

I glanced up at Brian. There was an odd look on his face, and his forehead was creased like he was deep in thought. He'd not been working so much in the few days before Christmas, but he still seemed a little off. I was worried about him. Whenever I tried to talk to him about it, he told me it was the stress of his job but I had a niggling feeling there was something else going on.

"Is everything okay?" I asked.

"Yeah." He didn't sound very convincing.

"You've been really quiet recently."

"I'm fine." He leaned closer and kissed my forehead.

Someone passed a bunch of song sheets along the row and the choir launched into *Little Donkey*. I wasn't convinced Brian *was* fine but now wasn't the time to quiz him further.

"Look!" Callum sidled up next to me and pointed to a man coming around the corner of the church with a real live donkey.

I turned to Linda. "You didn't say there'd be animals!" She smiled proudly at me. Animals would certainly liven things up.

After forty-five minutes, I was completely engrossed and loving every minute. I was singing at the top of my lungs and I could almost feel the joy in the air. It was magical. There'd been a real life Mary and Joseph (Joseph was played by Linda's husband, George!) and even a real baby for baby Jesus. There was something very touching about singing *While Shepherd's Watched* as real sheep appeared with their shepherds. I was grateful that it was starting to go dark because I suddenly felt tears sting my eyes.

As the choir quietly started to sing *Silent Night* I felt a tingling on my cheeks and looked up to see snowflakes falling around us. I got so choked up I couldn't sing. I leaned further into Brian and pulled Callum tighter to me.

"Are you crying, Marie?" Callum asked me with a cheeky grin.

"No." I stared ahead, blinking furiously. I could feel him and Brian looking at me with big grins.

"Yes, you are!" Callum said.

"It's just so magical." I sniffed and gave him a big kiss on the cheek. He squirmed to get away from me and moved away to stand with Sophie and Jeff.

Brian gave me a kiss on the cheek and I took a deep breath and composed myself so I could join in with the last verse of *Silent Night*.

"Linda, this is the best Christmas Eve I've ever had!" I beamed at her when the service was over.

She pulled me in for a hug. "I told you you'd enjoy it."

There was a lot of hugging going on, partly to wish each other a Merry Christmas and partly to exchange body heat. My toes were completely numb and I was sure I didn't have long before hypothermia set in.

Our little group huddled together and began walking towards the main road.

"Thanks for coming!" Ted called as he overtook us at a good pace. He glanced back. "Anyone fancy joining me at the pub?"

We exchanged looks before collectively agreeing.

"It's at the top of the hill." He pointed to a building on its own all lit up at the top of the road. "I'm going to have to hurry though, I'm freezing. See you up there!"

"We'll have to get Callum home so we'll see you in the morning," Jake said.

"You go," Michael said. "I'll go with Callum. Just don't get too drunk. And make sure you're home before Santa comes!" He winked and gave us all a wave.

Brian dropped back to walk with Jake, while Sophie came and took my arm.

"That was surprisingly alright, wasn't it?" she said.

"Yes! It was amazing. I love that we're all together and it just feels so Christmassy. The songs and the snow and everyone huddled together."

She gave me a funny look.

"What?" I asked.

"You're not knocked up are you?"

"What? No!"

"Really? You keep getting all teary and pathetic."

"It's not pathetic. I had a lovely time, that's all. That doesn't mean I'm pregnant!"

"Are you sure?"

"Yes!"

"Good to know!" Brian called from behind us. I glanced back and my stomach did a flip at the sight of him and his mischievous smile.

"And if I was, I wouldn't be announcing it like this, would I? I might give Brian a bit of a heads up."

"So we still don't know for sure?" Sophie asked.

"I just told you, I'm not!"

"But then you said that even if you were, you'd deny it until you'd told Brian. Therefore we still don't really know." She wriggled out of my grip and made a run for it.

I shook my head and laughed, then picked up my pace as we neared the pub.

Chapter 15

From the outside it appeared to be a sleepy little pub, trussed up nicely with pretty Christmas lights. Inside, the first thing I noticed was the warmth; it was so lovely. The next thing I noticed was the Christmas music playing; also really lovely. Then, from out of nowhere, an older gentleman in a suit planted a wet kiss on my lips. Not so lovely.

"Steady on!" Brian said, behind me.

The man moved on to kiss him too, and I caught sight of the mistletoe in his hand. I laughed at Brian's stunned expression. After releasing Brian, he proceeded to kiss Jake.

"That's quite a welcome committee," Brian said before his eyes went wide. I turned to follow his gaze.

I Wish it Could be Christmas Everyday was blaring round the pub and in the middle of it all was Linda. She was standing on the bar, microphone in hand, singing her heart out. She was looking fairly nun-like in her calf-length grey skirt and cream blouse so it was amusing to see her pause to take a sip of the shot which was handed to her. She beamed when she saw me.

"Marie!" she shouted and beckoned me over. She must have only been in the pub two minutes before me so I couldn't quite fathom how she was already drunk and dancing on the bar.

Hands on my back pushed me towards the bar and I laughed, shaking my head. A bearded man in a Santa hat handed me a shot.

"Thanks!" I hesitantly knocked it back, grimacing slightly as it went down.

"Come on!" Sophie pulled me closer to the bar and then she climbed up via a stool.

I was still shaking my head when two beefy-looking guys appeared at either side of me and lifted me effortlessly up onto the bar. Sophie and Linda grinned at me and I laughed loudly before downing a second shot. Then I joined in with the dancing. It wasn't going to end well.

As the song came to an end, I climbed down and made my way across the pub to find Brian. It took a while, what with everyone was wishing me a happy Christmas and offering to buy me drinks. I finally arrived at the table in the window where Brian, Jake, and Jeff had settled themselves.

"Where's George?" I asked.

"Playing with the locals." Jeff nodded to the left. George was at the next table engrossed in a game of dominos. He was wearing brown corduroy trousers and a grey cardigan over a green checked shirt. He fitted in nicely with his fellow domino players. I still wasn't convinced he liked any of us, so it didn't surprise me that he'd managed to avoid sitting with us.

"There's something for everyone here." I perched myself on Brian's lap and pushed my hand into his lovely dark hair as I gave him a long kiss on the lips.

"Hey!" Jeff nudged us. "Get a room, will you?!"

"The shots went to my head." I took a sip of the pint I'd acquired on my walk through the pub. "I can see why Ted was in such a rush. It's brilliant in here." I looked round the pub to see groups of people chatting and laughing away. A few people were dancing, and the atmosphere was amazing.

A huge guy in a Santa suit arrived at our table with a tray of shots and deposited them on the table with a "Ho! Ho! Ho!" We dutifully drank up.

"Wahey!" Sophie jeered as she joined us. "How much fun is this place? Cheers, Father Ted!" She raised her glass and Ted gave us a wave. "I'm going for a wee," she told us as she moved away again.

I hurried after her.

"What's going on with you and Jeff?" I asked once we reached the comparative quiet of the Ladies'. My plan to keep out of it hadn't lasted long.

"He's annoying me." She raised her voice as we headed into the only two toilet stalls. "He's like a little lap dog and he's so possessive and jealous. He suddenly needs to know where I am at all times and, well, he's just a bit boring, isn't he?"

"No! He's not boring; he's lovely. Don't you dare mess him about."

"Whose side are you on?"

"No ones. If it's not working out, split up with him, but I'm just saying, don't mess him about."

"He's just such a nice guy, it's annoying. I want a bit of excitement."

"Jeff is fun! Remember he used to play all those practical jokes, like sending us into fat club instead of speed dating? He's funny."

"He used to be. I just want to have fun, but he's

always offering to help Mum with the kids, and he wants to stay in and watch TV at the weekends."

"Hey!" I said. "Brian and I stay in and watch TV at weekends." I opened the toilet door and caught her eye in the mirror as she fiddled with her hair.

"Yes, but you're old and boring." She grinned at me. "And even though Brian is all boring and loved up, you can still see he's a bit of a bad boy deep down. He's got that glint in his eye. Jeff seems to have lost his wild side all together."

"So you're going to split up with him?"

"Well not on bloody Christmas Eve! What kind of heartless monster do you think I am? Plus, I won't get a present if I dump him now." She looked at me and changed the subject abruptly. "What's up with Brian?"

"I don't know. Work stuff I think." Apparently it wasn't only me who noticed his mood.

"He's quiet. I don't like it. Do you want me to talk to him? I can find out what's bothering him."

"No. I'm perfectly capable of talking to him, thanks."

"Clearly!" she said cheekily.

I followed her out of the toilets. Jeff was by the bar, chatting to a couple of girls. I'm not sure if Sophie didn't notice or was just pretending not to. I wouldn't put it past her to start a bar brawl.

"Sophie!" Jeff called, catching up with us by our table. "Can I talk to you outside for a minute?"

"Why? It's bloody freezing out there."

"Just for a minute," he pleaded. I felt sorry for him. Sophie ignored him and took a seat next to Brian.

"Fine." Jeff looked suitably annoyed. "I'm going

home. I wanted to split up with you privately but I guess I can just do it here."

"You're splitting up with me?" Sophie asked. I winced at the shock on her face.

He shrugged and reached for his jacket from the back of a chair. "I don't know why you look so surprised. This is clearly not working anymore. I'm amazed you've stuck at it this long. You seem to be constantly pissed off with me. Sorry everyone." He looked around at us. "Have a great Christmas!"

He left and Sophie ran after him.

Jake raised his glass. "Well cheers everyone!"

"I had no clue Jeff was that brave," Brian said jokily. "And on Christmas Eve. It's a bit mean really."

"She's going to be a nightmare." I sighed and then looked up at Brian and Jake staring at me. "Oh, don't look at me like that! You know I meant to say something sympathetic and sincere. Sometimes things come out wrong." They were glaring at me. "She will be a nightmare though, and it'll be me who bears the brunt of it. She'll be crying on my shoulder all Christmas."

Brian rolled his eyes at me. "Jeff should really have thought about how this would affect you, shouldn't he? Selfish prick!"

I gave him a shove, then stood to give Sophie a hug when she came back in.

She ignored me completely and snuggled into Brian. "The stupid idiot dumped me. And at Christmas." Tears streamed down her face and Brian hugged her, giving me a smug look over her head.

She'd be crying to me later. Definitely. The long-term effects would land squarely on my shoulders.

A nervous-looking George appeared next to me. "Could I ask you a favour?" he said meekly. "Could you possibly fetch Linda for me? I think we should be getting home now."

"Fetch her yourself," Sophie snapped at him. "What did your last slave die of?"

He cowered slightly and looked across the pub. "Well I just thought it might be better if one of you could get her."

I scanned the room until my eyes settled on Linda. She was sitting on Santa's knee with her head thrown back in laughter.

"I see your point, George. I'll get her."

I made my way across the pub, avoiding drunken old men with mistletoe as I went.

"Come on, Linda! Time to go home."

"Marie!" Linda spluttered through her laughter. "He just ... he just … he said something really funny! Tell Marie that funny thing!"

Someone slid a tray of shots onto the table and Linda picked one up. "Try one of these, Marie. They're great."

"I think we need to go. George is waiting for you."

"Let him wait! It's Christmas! Have a drink with me and stop being such a party-pooper."

"Come on, love!" Santa pulled me onto his spare knee. "Tell me what you want from Santa. I presume you've been a good girl this year?"

Linda collapsed into uncontrollable belly laughter, snorting occasionally and getting redder by the second.

I sighed and grabbed a shot. A cheer went up as I

downed it. There's something really encouraging about people cheering when you drink. I reached for another.

"Ho! Ho! Ho!" Santa laughed and I looked at Linda before laughing so hard I almost fell off his lap.

"You're right, Linda, he is funny!"

I'm not sure how much time passed before Brian came and towered over us. I jumped up and into his arms, wobbling slightly.

"Sorry, Santa, but I'm going to have to take these ladies off your hands." Brian was greeted by a collective groan from our new friends.

Linda pointed a finger at him accusingly. "Party-pooper!"

He reached out and pulled her up.

As Brian manoeuvred the pair of us across the pub we shouted, "Happy Christmas!" to everyone we passed.

"Here, George. One wife, as requested." Brian handed Linda over when we hit the cold air outside.

"Finally," Sophie said huffily. "You did a better job than Marie."

I turned to face her. "What is your problem?"

"I just got dumped and then had to wait in the cold for you. That's my problem!"

"Well excuse me for having fun. Happy flipping Christmas!"

"I think it's time to split up and head home," Brian said. "George can you drop Sophie off? We'll share a taxi with Jake." We shouted our goodbyes as we split up.

"I hope we can find a taxi," Jake said, as we headed down the hill to the main road. "It is Christmas Eve."

"Never fear!" I said theatrically as I pulled out my phone.

Chapter 16

"Happy Christmas, Dave!" I stumbled into the taxi. "This is Dave!" I told Brian and Jake, even though they'd met before. Dave worked for the local taxi firm and was my favourite driver.

"Happy Christmas, love! I haven't seen you in a while."

"No, I've got a Brian now and he drives me places. Very handy!"

"I just hope we don't go out of business!"

"You're funny, Dave." I hiccupped. "Brian wants me to take driving lessons too. How silly is that? He tried to teach me himself, but we only managed one lesson. It did not go well. Not well at all!" I smiled and hiccupped again.

"Not the best day," Brian agreed.

"I'm not a natural, am I, Brian?"

"I wouldn't say that." He paused and grinned. "Not to your face anyway."

"You'll get there." Jake was encouraging as always. "A few lessons and you'll be fine."

"You're right." I nudged Brian playfully. "I just need a proper instructor. I'm sure I'd pick it up in no time." I leaned into the front to talk to Jake. "What time are you coming round tomorrow? I can't keep track of everyone."

"Carol's working tonight so we said we'd wait until she's up and have some time with her before we come over. Best for Callum that way." Callum's mum, Carol, worked in a bar. She was a single mum, and was quite unreliable so Callum spent most of his time with Jake.

I nodded. "Did you invite Carol to our place?"

"She's working again tomorrow afternoon so she can't. She appreciated the offer though." He smiled at me and I think we both knew that she wouldn't have appreciated the offer. She was in one of her wild streaks and wouldn't be keen to hang out with us boring people.

At one point, Carol and Sophie had been friends. Sophie used to bring her out with us sometimes, but that hadn't happened for a while and Sophie seemed to have given up on her. Sophie adored Callum so I think it was hard for her to see Carol letting him down so often.

"It's a shame Michael can't come," Brian said as we pulled up outside Jake's house. Everyone approved of Jake's boyfriend, Michael. He was easy-going and doted on both Callum and Jake. They were a sweet unconventional little family.

"He's got to cook Christmas dinner for the old people at the home. It's actually a nice shift to work. It's all very festive. The old dears like a good knees up! He's taking my mum with him. She goes every year, even if I'm not working. I think she's getting excited about the time when she can move into an old people's home. She loves it there. Anyway, I'll see you tomorrow!"

We shouted "Happy Christmas!" as he closed the

door.

"What do you think, then?" Dave asked. "White Christmas or not?"

"No," I said. The few flakes at the carol service hadn't lasted long.

"Yes," Brian said. "Definitely. I asked Santa for snow. And I've been a really good boy!" He gave me a cheeky smile.

"Well," I said. "Sometimes you've been a bit naughty too. Remember the other night ..." He clamped a hand over my mouth and smiled at Dave who was looking at us in the rear view mirror.

Dave laughed as he pulled up in front of the house.

"Have a lovely Christmas, Dave!" I stumbled out of the car and up the steps to the front door.

"The house looks lovely," I said when I landed ungracefully on the couch. "So pretty!" The Christmas tree looked wonderful in the corner of the living room.

"Shall we have a drink?" Brian asked.

"There's a slight chance I'm already drunk ..."

He appeared next to me a couple of minutes later and handed me a bottle of beer. "Happy Christmas, soon-to-be Mrs Connor!"

"Happy Christmas." Putting the beer down on the coffee table, I kissed his cheek, then leaned my head back on the couch. The room was spinning slightly. I definitely didn't need anymore alcohol.

Brian took a long swig of his beer. "Do you think we'll be married this time next year?"

I groaned. "You're not going to start on at me about the wedding are you?"

"I just wondered if it's ever going to happen."

"It will definitely happen. I'm not sure what the rush is?"

"I was thinking about what Sophie was saying about you being pregnant."

"I'm not!"

"That's clear judging by your alcohol consumption. But it got me thinking, and it wouldn't be so bad if you were, would it?"

"Brian!" I was far too drunk for this conversation. "Let's worry about getting married first and then we can think about babies."

"Okay. So let's get married."

I wiggled my ring finger at him. "I already agreed to it!"

His eyes narrowed. I'd been dodging the conversation for too long. His patience was getting less and less saint-like.

"Is this what's been bothering you?" I asked.

"What do you mean?"

"You've just been a bit distant and quiet. I thought you were stressed with work."

He sighed and leaned forward, resting his elbows on his knees. "Work has been pretty full on, but it also bothers me that you avoid talking about the wedding. I get the feeling you don't really want to marry me."

I tensed at his words and hated how vulnerable he looked while he waited for me to respond. I wasn't sure what to say though.

"Silence really does speak volumes, doesn't it?" He spat the words bitterly at me, getting up from the couch.

I caught his hand and pulled him back. "I do want to marry you." He raised his eyebrows at me. My thoughts were jumbled and I couldn't think straight. I wondered for a moment whether I did want to marry him. I loved him and I couldn't imagine my life without out him but I just wasn't sure we needed to make a big fuss. Things were fine as they were.

"Can we talk about this another time? Maybe when we've not been drinking and it's not the early hours of the morning."

He rubbed the back of his neck. "I already tried that approach."

"I'm just a bit sick of people asking me about the wedding all the time. It's as though people think that's all I would be interested in talking about."

"But most people would be interested in talking about it. Most people would be excited, and dying to talk about it and plan it."

"Maybe I don't want a wedding," I blurted out. My eyes filled with tears as Brian moved his hands to his face, rubbing his eyes.

"You couldn't have mentioned this before?"

I silently contemplated what I'd said. I didn't know that's how I felt until I said it. It was true though. I didn't want a wedding.

"I didn't really know. Everyone just kept talking about the wedding and you keep pushing me. It's all a bit much."

"I'm not pushing you into anything. I asked you to marry me. You said yes. Now you've changed your mind?"

"No! Of course I want to marry you, but that doesn't mean we need a big wedding." I felt the tension in his body as I put a hand on his shoulder. "Brian, I don't want to argue with you. I'm tired and drunk and it's Christmas."

"Happy Christmas!" His voice oozed sarcasm and he held up his beer bottle in a toast before drinking the last of it. "I'm going to bed."

I followed him up and crawled into bed beside him. "Don't be angry with me." I trailed a hand over his chest. It was Christmas Eve and I'd been perfectly merry until he brought up the subject of the wedding. I didn't was us to go to sleep annoyed with each other.

He frowned and didn't say anything. I poked the corner of his mouth and he swatted my hand away.

"I just want to make you smile," I said, doing the same again.

He caught my hand and smirked. "You can't just push my mouth into a smile!"

"I think I can." I did it again with my other hand and he laughed as he squirmed away from me.

"You're crazy," he said.

"I'm drunk," I corrected him. "And I don't like you being grumpy. You shouldn't start serious conversations with me after we've been in the pub all night."

"You might have a point," he said, pulling me into his arms.

"Smile and I'll forgive you."

He grinned widely. I glanced at the clock on the bedside table. It was after midnight.

"Happy Christmas, Brian." I snuggled happily into his chest.

"Happy Christmas," he whispered.

Chapter 17

I squinted when the sunlight hit my eyes. My body refused to move.

"Happy Christmas!" Brian sang far too cheerfully.

"Nothing is happy, Brian, I'm dying."

"I think that might just be a little hangover."

"Nope. Definitely dying."

"That's a shame because Santa brought you presents. Plus, you invited loads of people round."

"They invited themselves," I corrected him. "Oh, the oven should be on … turn the oven on." I managed to lift an arm up and point in what I thought was the vague direction of the kitchen.

A wave of nausea hit me when Brian seated himself next to me, making the mattress sink.

"Oven," I moaned.

"Already did it."

"Good. How can I cook Christmas dinner in this state?"

"I guess you'll need help," he said lightly.

"It's difficult though."

"Not that difficult since you bought everything ready prepared. It just needs sticking in the oven."

"Yeah but you have to get the timings right. That's the key. Linda told me."

"I'm sure I'll figure it out."

"But it needs to look like I didn't buy stuff pre-prepared and that I've slaved over it and done an amazing job."

"Well that bit could be difficult."

"You'll manage."

The contents of my stomach threatened to reappear when Brian stood. I had to drag myself off the bed and make a run for the bathroom. After a horrific five minutes, I'd rid myself of the remnants of the previous night's alcohol and felt slightly more human.

I perched pathetically on a stool at the island in the kitchen and gratefully accepted a cup of coffee from Brian.

"Sorry about the wedding stuff," I said. "It came out wrong."

"It's okay, I shouldn't have snapped. Let's just enjoy Christmas. We can talk about it later." Brian turned to put the turkey in the oven. Part of me felt like chatting to him about it. I knew I owed him an explanation and that it would be better to talk it through and clear the air. It was hard to know what to say about it though. I didn't really know how I felt about it.

"I do love you." I wrapped my hands around the coffee mug. "And I definitely want to marry you."

He came and kissed my lips. "That's all that matters then. We can figure everything else out later."

"Father Ted has a lot to answer for," I said as Brian moved back to the stove. "I had this idea of a perfect Christmas morning, just the two of us. But now I feel like death. This was not part of the plan. And what happened with Sophie? Did I argue with her?"

Memories were stirring in my head.

"Not really. You were both getting a bit feisty. We split you up just in time."

"Oh, no. Jeff split up with her." It suddenly came back to me. "Oh, she'll be so grumpy."

"Yeah. That was your drunk reaction too."

"Well I'd be more concerned if she hadn't been planning on splitting up with *him*. It's the fact that he got in first that's going to cause a problem. She'll be unbearable. I mean, honestly, how dare he split up with her? I guess that means we're one less for Christmas dinner now too?"

"You were the one complaining you wanted a quiet Christmas. Now you're concerned about numbers dropping?"

I made a face at him in reply.

"Come on." He pulled me up from the stool and I followed him into the living room. The fire was roaring and the tree was all lit up.

"You forgot the Christmas music," I told him, with a cheeky grin.

He turned the radio on and then handed me a beautifully wrapped little box, complete with ribbon. I opened it excitedly to find a stunning silver charm bracelet.

"Like it?" he asked as he fastened it for me.

"I love it." I looked closer and smiled. "Some of the charms are a bit random."

"Well, this is a little heart so you remember how much I love you."

"And a bike?" I laughed.

"That signifies the first time we met and you hitched a ride on the back of my bike. Nutter!"

"I like the little Statue of Liberty."

"To remind you of our New York trip," he said.

"And the *F*?" I fingered the little charm.

"Fat club! Or friends ... you decide."

"It's perfect." I looked at it in amazement and wondered how I'd managed to end up with Brian.

"You'll have to wait a while for yours," I said.

"You didn't forget, did you?"

"No! It's just not quite as good as this." I'd had a horrible time trying to decide what to get him and I still wasn't convinced he'd like it. I reached up and kissed him.

He pulled back abruptly and looked me in the eyes.

"We are okay, aren't we?" he asked.

"Yes." My chest felt suddenly tight. "Why wouldn't we be?"

He shook his head. "I don't know."

"You said we should just enjoy Christmas and talk properly later."

"About the wedding?"

My heart began to race as I looked into his eyes. "What else?"

"I don't know. I feel like things have been strange between us and ..." He dropped his gaze and shifted his weight awkwardly.

"And what?" I asked.

A loud knocking came at the door. Brian turned away quickly, seemingly glad of the interruption.

"Brian." I grabbed his arm and pulled him back towards me. "You're acting strange, and it's freaking me out."

He closed his eyes and rubbed his temples. "Sorry, I'm just stressed out." He finally managed to look at me.

I pulled him in for a hug. "I love you."

"I love you too," he said before following the sound of more banging at the door. Tears sprang to my eyes as he moved away from me. I had no idea what was going on. Something was definitely bothering him and I was fairly sure it wasn't just about the wedding.

I heard Sophie's harsh voice when Brian opened the front door. "Where's Marie?" She was probably going to have a go at me about last night. I dabbed at my eyes and took a deep breath.

"Marie!" Her tone changed when she came into the living room. "Happy Christmas!"

"Happy Christmas!" I returned her hug uncertainly. "Everything okay?"

"Of course. It's Christmas!"

"You're very lively. Aren't you hungover?"

"I was! You should have seen the state of me at five o'clock this morning when the kids were jumping all over me. I was not a pretty sight. A couple of bacon butties perked me right up. How crazy was the pub last night? I can see why Linda goes to church now; Father Ted's such a laugh. He cracked me up! Is the turkey in the oven?" I followed her into the kitchen where Brian was working away. I was amazed by Sophie's energy. I caught Brian's eye and we exchanged an awkward smile. It did nothing to put my mind at ease.

"What's this?" Sophie held up the foil container of chopped carrots and looked accusingly at me. "Why is all the food in take-away dishes?"

"They're not a take-away dishes," I said. "I just

121

prepared everything yesterday and put it in the foil containers to save washing up later. It's a little trick that Linda taught me." I added the last bit to make it sound more believable.

"Did she also teach you to seal it and put price labels on?"

"Nope. I thought that one up all by myself. Anyway, I'm going to have a shower. Stop picking on me."

Sophie followed me. "I'm coming too."

"We're not that close," I said.

"No, silly! I'll just chat to you through the door. I need to talk to you."

"Did you talk to Jeff?" I asked.

In the bathroom I left the door slightly ajar.

"I rang him this morning and we both apologised. He said he shouldn't have dumped me on Christmas Eve - which he shouldn't have – but he got fed up of things the way they were." She raised her voice over the sound of the water. "I said it was mostly my fault for getting angry at him about things instead of talking to him."

"That's very mature. I'll be honest, I'm quite surprised. I thought it would be a huge drama."

"No. I don't have time for drama."

I couldn't help but laugh.

"Well not that kind of drama!" She laughed with me. "I told him we should have a break over Christmas and then talk things through next week. We'll definitely still be friends, even if we're not together."

"It's a shame he won't be here today though."

"Wasn't it you who wanted to have Christmas with

Brian and none of the rest of us? I thought you'd be thanking me for cutting down the numbers."

"I was just winding you up." I spoke loudly as I rinsed shampoo out of my hair. "Of course I wanted to spend Christmas with everyone."

"You're a terrible liar. Hurry up in there. You're wasting the day!"

I turned the shower off and wrapped a towel around me.

"Look what Brian bought me." I showed off the bracelet as I came out of the bathroom.

"I've already seen it. I wanted to check he didn't get you something crap so I made him show it to me. I approved. Now hurry up and get dressed and let's get on with Christmas!"

She bounded back downstairs with her usual energy, leaving me to get dressed in peace.

Chapter 18

"Everything okay?" I asked Brian when I joined him in the kitchen.

"Yeah. Sorry about before."

"It's fine." Clearly things weren't fine but I was keen to leave awkward conversations for another day. "What shall I do?"

He pulled a Santa hat onto my head and kissed me. "It's all under control."

"I have to do something." I gazed up at him. "I'm going to take all the credit."

"I'll make sure I burn everything then."

I moved to the stove and stirred the gravy.

"Your mum and Aunt Kath are here," he said. "Ellie brought a cheesecake." He grinned at me and I sighed. I loved that he got on so well with my slightly crazy mum. I still found it weird that he called her Ellie; she was Eleanor to everyone else but she insisted Brian called her Ellie.

"I told her she didn't need to bring anything. I wish she'd listened for once."

"I'm sure it's delicious!"

"After almost thirty years of eating Mum's food, I'm sure it will be anything but delicious!" When it came to Mum's cooking there were various levels of bizarre and disgusting; delicious never came into it.

"There you are," Mum said as she and Aunt Kath walked in from the living room. "Slaving away in the kitchen, you poor thing! We've been chatting to Sophie. Happy Christmas!"

"Happy Christmas, Mum!" I looked her up and down. Christmas was a good time for her. She could dress as an elf and get away with it. It was slightly awkward in August when she just had the urge to dress like an elf.

"Open your present." She handed me a bulky package and I braced myself as I opened it.

"Oh, wow! Lovely!" I held up the green jumper which looked about three sizes too big for me. I turned it towards Brian to show him the huge Santa face that was sewn on the front, very clearly a homemade item. Santa's beard was made of white pieces of wool, which hung from his chin to below the bottom of the jumper.

"Try it on," Mum said.

I pulled it on over my lovely new top, thinking of all the time I'd wasted choosing something nice to wear.

"Don't worry, Brian, there's one for you too!" Mum said.

"You had me panicking for a minute there, Ellie!" He opened his parcel to find his jumper. It had a snowman on the front. Definitely an improvement on mine, although the carrot-shaped nose sticking out from his chest looked a bit dodgy.

"Oh, look!" I said. "The dog's got one too." Little Rex came running into the kitchen wearing a red jumper with white cuffs and collar. It was way more stylish than our jumpers. He wagged his tail and ran straight back out again.

"Hello?" Jake's voice boomed through to us.

"Come in!" I shouted and then glanced at Brian. "They're early. I thought they weren't coming until later. I bet something happened with Carol."

I headed towards the front door. "Happy Christmas!"

"Happy Christmas!" Jake replied. I gave him a big hug and glanced at Callum who was staring at his feet. I hated it when he was like this; it was like his gorgeous happy personality was eaten up by his shy, vulnerable side. It was always his Mum that brought it on.

"Happy Christmas, Callum!" I said excitedly. I'd learned to carry on as normal and he'd soon come back to us. "Look at this …" I pointed at my jumper and shimmied a little to make the beard move. "Ho! Ho! Ho!"

Callum looked up briefly and I noticed how red his eyes were. Jake gave me a pained look.

"We're not sure yet if it's a jumper or a dress," Brian said as he appeared behind me. "What do you think of mine?" He stuck his hand up his jumper and attacked me with the carrot nose.

"You both look crazy, but what's new?" Sophie came out of the living room, laughing. "Callum! Finally I have someone fun to hang out with!" She moved to put an arm around him and cover him with kisses.

He struggled to get away from her and a small smile crept onto his lips.

"Come and look at the dog," she said. "He's dressed like Santa. I've been trying to decide how to make him a little white beard."

"What happened?" I asked Jake quietly as Callum followed Sophie into the living room.

"Carol didn't come home last night and she's not answering her phone. I guess she passed out somewhere. Sorry we're early but Michael was going to work and taking my mum. I couldn't face sitting with Callum, waiting to see if she turned up, which she most likely wouldn't."

"No problem for us," I said. "Poor Callum though. I thought things were getting better but it all seems to be going down hill again, doesn't it?"

Callum's head appeared around the living room door. "Sophie said you got take-away for Christmas dinner. You didn't, did you?"

"Of course not. Don't believe anything Sophie tells you."

There was another knock at the door. Jake opened it to Linda and George.

"I feel terrible," Linda said as she hugged me. "I don't know what got into me last night."

"I think that might have been tequila."

"Oh, Marie, don't! Don't even say the word. It turns my stomach." She looked pale and pathetic.

"Go and sit down. Have a drink and you'll feel fine."

"I can't, Marie. I'm never drinking alcohol again."

I laughed as she handed me a shopping bag of desserts and moved towards the living room.

"Brian's in charge of drinks," I said loudly. "I'll be slaving away in the kitchen if anyone needs me."

"Do you want a glass of this?" Brian asked me as he pulled a bottle of bubbly from the fridge and moved things around to make room for Linda's trifle.

"It's a bit early still. I'm not fully recovered from last night yet."

"It's midday," he said.

"Really? Go on then." I turned down the heat where the potatoes were threatening to boil over and moved the gravy to the back. I peered into the oven and everything looked good. So far I was doing well.

Sophie was mumbling to herself when she walked into the kitchen with her mobile in her hand. "If I could find her, I might just kill her. That stupid cow! How can she do that to Callum?"

"Are you trying to call Carol?" I asked.

"Yeah, but she's not answering. She's so bloody selfish." Sophie moved over to me and leaned against the sideboard. "It's not fair, all she has to do is turn up. Why can't she manage that?" Her voice caught and tears fell down her cheeks.

"Oh, Sophie." I pulled her to me. "Don't let her upset you. You can't do anything about it. Just be there for Callum like you always are."

Brian came and put his arms around us both. "He'll be okay, Sophie. You're amazing with him. You always cheer him up."

"The dog is so cute–" Callum wandered into the kitchen and stopped when he saw the three of us huddled together.

We broke apart quickly and Sophie frantically wiped at her eyes with her sleeves.

"What's wrong?" Callum asked.

"Jeff dumped me," she said.

He put his arms round her waist and gave her a big squeeze. "What an idiot."

"Exactly. His loss!" She gave him a quick hug and then composed herself and moved to the fridge.

"Look at this …" She opened the door to change the subject. "Yummy chocolate cheesecake!"

"Mmmm!" Callum's eyes went wide. He loved all things chocolate.

"Marie's mum made it!" Sophie said.

"Oh!" He recoiled. "What's in it?"

She grinned at him. "We'll find out later!"

"Hey!" I closed the fridge door. "I'm sure it's delicious. Now get out of the kitchen and stop annoying me." They left and I saw them exchanging glances and making vomit faces. To be fair, one of Mum's previous cheesecakes was a sponge cake with lumps of cheddar cheese in it, but I still struggled when anyone else criticised my mum.

I loved to watch them together though; Sophie was like a big sister to Callum. She always looked out for him.

"There's never a dull moment, is there?" I said to Brian.

I carried Linda's Christmas cake into the dining room. It was adorned with perfect snowmen figures and looked spectacular.

I was quite proud of what we'd done to the dining room. We'd set it all up the previous afternoon - extending the table to make more room and covering it with a beautiful Christmassy tablecloth. There was a little wreath with candles for the centrepiece and I'd even got a small Christmas tree on a table in the corner of the room.

"I brought a Christmas pudding too in the end," Linda said, joining me in the dining room. "It's just a shop-bought one though."

Sophie appeared beside me. "Where are the table presents?"

"I told you, if you want extra presents you have to organise that yourself."

"I know! I was kidding. I'll fetch them." She ran out of the room.

"Table presents?" Linda asked.

"It's Sophie's idea."

"You need to have presents for everyone at the table," Sophie explained as she pulled little gifts out of a bag and set one at each place. "Then it's easy to get everyone to come and sit down to eat."

"Isn't the food tempting enough?" Linda asked. "Marie's cooking isn't that bad, is it?"

"Hey!" I pretended to be offended.

"My mum always does it," Sophie said. "It's to get the kids away from their toys to sit down and eat. But it's a tradition now. I can't sit down to Christmas dinner without a present at the table. Where are the crackers, Marie?"

"Oh, I almost forgot." I turned and retrieved the box of Christmas crackers from the cupboard in the dresser and passed them to Sophie. She added one to each place.

"It looks so lovely," Linda said, beaming. "And the food smells great."

"The food!" I panicked for a moment before looking through to the kitchen. Brian was hovering over the oven. "All under control, love?" I shouted. He replied with a thumbs up.

"I better go and check on him," I told Linda and Sophie quietly. "He's got no clue what he's doing."

I caught them exchanged knowing looks. "He doesn't! It's all down to me this Christmas dinner. Don't let him trick you into thinking he's doing everything. He just keeps waltzing into the kitchen to make everyone think he's Mr Perfect!"

Their smug little smiles never wavered. I gave up trying to convince them and went into the kitchen.

"Here, put this on." Brian handed me an apron. "It might help to fool people into thinking you're the chef."

I glared at him but took the apron and tied it round my waist. It actually wasn't a bad plan. I reached into the cupboard and stuck my finger into a packet of flour and then smudged it on to my cheek. "Now I really look the part, don't I?"

Brian grinned and turned the radio up, taking my hand and giving me a twirl before dancing me around the kitchen.

"You're really quite odd," he said.

"Thanks!"

"It's okay. I love you anyway."

"Well that's big of you." I wriggled as his snowman nose dug into my ribs. "This is ridiculous." I pulled on it and it came off in my hand. "Oh, no!" I panicked as Brian chuckled. "It's not funny; Mum will be upset." I couldn't help but laugh a bit too though.

"Sod it!" I threw it on to the sideboard. "Food's ready everyone!"

Chapter 19

There was some bustle as everyone found their places at the table and opened their little presents from Sophie; an array of sample beauty products.

"Thanks a lot, Sophie!" I couldn't help but smile when I unwrapped my anti-aging cream. "This should be really useful."

"You're welcome. It should help a bit with the wrinkles." We were both smiling as Brian came in with the turkey on the platter. It smelled delicious and was met with groans of approval.

George got up and moved towards Brian. He hovered for a while, clearing his throat nervously.

"You okay, George?" Brian asked.

"I need to …" He gestured the turkey. "It's my thing. I always carve the turkey."

Brian stopped, carving knife in hand.

"You don't get a special request, George," Sophie said. "It's one per family. Marie said so." I'd put my foot down after getting numerous emails with more and more demands.

George glared at her.

"I didn't make a special request in the end," Linda said. "So this is ours. George really wants to carve the turkey."

"Isn't that like taking all the glory?" Sophie said.

"Shouldn't Brian carve since he slaved away in the kitchen all morning?"

"I did the cooking actually," I told them quickly. "Not that I want to carve the turkey. I'm just saying it wasn't all Brian." They all looked at me with their annoying little smiles. I was still wearing the apron so I'm not sure why they didn't believe me.

"It's fine," Brian said, relinquishing the carving knife.

"I think it's a bit rude," Sophie muttered. She was never very nice to George.

"Everyone is allowed a special request," Linda told her.

"Do we have this in writing though? Because all requests were supposed to be made prior to Christmas Day and in writing."

"Sophie." George's voice bounced around the room, strong and authoritative. "Shut up!" He glared at her and the presence of the carving knife made him look outright menacing. I waited to see if Sophie would dare argue with him.

"Sorry, George," she mumbled.

His eyes lingered on Sophie for a moment before he turned his attention to the turkey. Linda had a funny little smile on her face.

I began filling my plate. "Tuck in, everyone."

"Crackers first!" Aunt Kath said excitedly. Everyone obediently reached for their Christmas crackers. The bangs were followed by a round of unfunny jokes and some swapping of gifts. Apparently Linda had been waiting months for a set of tiny screwdrivers to fix her reading glasses.

My mouth was starting to water. "Right, tuck in

then everyone!"

"Get your hats on," Jake said from his place next to Callum. I looked to see if he was being serious. Did I really have to wear a paper crown to eat my meal? I looked over at Sophie to see if she was going to object but she was filling up her plate. She had a green crown perched on her head.

"It keeps falling over my eyes," I said, hoping to get out of it.

"You'll survive!" Jake replied.

"I didn't actually receive this request in writing though."

Everyone stopped and looked at me like I had said something ridiculous, which clearly I had, but I didn't think it was much more ridiculous than having to wear a paper crown to eat.

"Put the crown on, Marie," Jake said calmly.

"But you already requested real gravy."

Sophie gave me a stern look. "Wearing the hat from the crackers isn't a special request, it's fairly standard. Now put it on and let's eat! Poor Brian's gone to all this effort and it's getting cold."

"It wasn't just Brian–" I caught the smirk on Sophie's face and couldn't help but smile as I put my crown on. Finally, I got to work loading up my plate.

Over the course of the meal, I zoned in and out of various conversations: Sophie jokingly telling Jake to go steady on the carbs; my mum discussing her dog-walking career with Brian; Callum dutifully answering Linda's questions about school.

"How are the wedding plans coming on?" George asked casually from his place opposite me.

The table fell silent and I felt Brian's eyes on me

as I tried to come up with an answer.

"We're still trying to figure out what we want to do," I replied vaguely.

"Have you set a date yet?" he asked, between mouthfuls of turkey.

"No, not yet."

"I was thinking," Mum said. "I could make you a dress if you want? I'm sure I could manage it. They're expensive to buy, you know."

Thankfully I didn't have any food in my mouth or I'm fairly sure I would've choked. I had visions of walking down the aisle in some crazy design of my mum's. Would she knit it? Would there be flashing lights? My mind boggled just imagining what she might come up with.

"It's okay, Mum. I think I'll treat myself."

"Okay. I already knitted a little cushion though. For the rings." I looked around the table. Everyone apart from Mum had their heads bowed, as though in prayer. I could distinctly see some shoulders shaking with silent laughter. My mum made a cushion for every occasion and apparently my wedding was no exception.

"Lovely, Mum. Thanks!"

"If there's anything else I can do, let me know." Mum beamed and I smiled weakly back at her.

"You need to get on and start looking at venues," Aunt Kath said as she chewed. "The nice places get booked up years in advance."

I shoved a forkful of roast potato in my mouth and smiled at her.

"I could even attach the cushion to Rex," Mum mused quietly. "He could walk down the aisle with the cushion and the rings on his back." I ignored Callum's giggles and stared at my mum. She was serious and looked really proud of her idea.

"The rings might fall off," Sophie said with a straight face.

"Oh no. I'd tie them on." Mum completely missed the fact that Sophie was teasing.

Sophie grinned at my mum and then at me. "In that case, it sounds like a great idea." If she were closer I would have kicked her.

"If you don't want me to make your dress, I could bake the wedding cake," Mum said enthusiastically. "You know I love to bake."

"No!" I snapped at her, silencing the giggles coming from Callum and Sophie. "I'm sorry, Mum, but I don't want you to make the cake or the dress. And I don't want the dog carrying the flipping rings." Mum swallowed hard as the room fell into silence.

"I'm sure there's lots you can help with, Ellie," Brian told her kindly. "Once we decide where and when we want to get married."

I felt like screaming that Mum wouldn't be able to help me because she was generally quite useless. I shoved more food in my mouth in an effort to avoid saying anything I would regret.

Sophie's eyes were on me and when I looked at her she broke the awkward silence.

"Did you not understand that the rings would be tied to the dog? What are you worried about? Nothing can go wrong."

She glared at me with only the slightest hint of a smirk; daring me not to laugh. I only managed a few seconds before my face broke into a smile.

Soon the room was filled with laughter.

Chapter 20

"Who's going first then?" I looked happily at all the presents under the tree.

Callum and Sophie jumped in, distributing gifts and shattering my illusions of an orderly present opening ceremony. Everyone eagerly tore at wrapping paper and my eyes darted round the room, trying to see what everyone got.

"I wonder who my Secret Santa was?!" Sophie held up my mum's signature gift; a handmade cushion with an *S* on the front.

Callum looked excited as he opened the new computer game that Brian had chosen for him. "Thank you!" he shouted to the room.

I opened my package to find a board game which I'd not heard of before. I flipped the box over to skim the instructions and then flashed Jake a smile. He knew I was a fan of board games and we often spent evenings playing games with Callum. I was yet to convince Callum that board games were better than his PlayStation but he seemed to enjoy them anyway.

Linda looked delighted with the colourful scarf I'd chosen for her. My gaze stopped at Sophie. There was a twinkle in her eye as she watched Jake unwrap his book-shaped present. His brow wrinkled and then his features softened. A laugh escaped him when he turned the book over.

"Who bought this?" he asked, holding it up.

"What is it?" Linda asked.

"It's called *Eat with Emily: A Mindful Eating Book*. Is this a joke or did she actually write a book?" Emily was the woman who ran the slimming club where we first met each other.

"She actually wrote it," Sophie said. "And that's a signed copy, Jake. It might be worth something one day."

Jake opened up the book. "To my dear friend, Jake. Always beware the fried breakfast. He is not your friend. Think thin, Jake! All my love, Emily." He looked suspiciously at Sophie.

"That was kind of her, wasn't it?" Sophie said.

"When you say it's a signed copy, Sophie ... I take it you signed this?"

"Well I did ask her but she wasn't keen on the idea."

"Let me see it." I reached for the book and turned it over to find a photo of Emily staring at the camera. It was quite creepy.

"Where did you find this?" I asked with a smile.

"She's selling them at the hotel," Sophie said. "Jeff told me about it."

"This looks interesting," Mum said. She was flipping through a big fat cookbook. I looked around to try and figure out who had bought it but no one was giving anything away.

"I don't like to stick to recipes usually, but I guess it's good to get some new ideas." She'd no doubt be pairing a starter with a dessert to make some whacky hybrid meal in no time.

"Awesome!" Callum said as he unwrapped a penknife. There was a big pile of presents in front of him.

"I guess you were better behaved than the rest of us this year, Callum. Santa seems to have a favourite." He grinned at me and I was glad he was back to his usual happy self and had managed to forget about his absent mother for a while. I think everyone had bought a gift for Callum as well as their Secret Santa gift.

While he continued opening presents, I slipped into the kitchen to put the kettle on. I took Mum's cheesecake out of the fridge, along with Linda's trifle and carried them into the dining room, placing them next to the Christmas cake. I picked up the Christmas pudding, happy to find it was microwavable.

I stood pondering the dessert selection for a while. My gaze lingered on Mum's cheesecake, which actually looked delicious. After almost thirty years of Mum's cooking, I couldn't be deceived by the look of it. There would definitely be some strange ingredients lurking in there. I was glad I had friends who accepted her with just the smallest amount of playful teasing, but sometimes I still wished she could be a bit more normal.

Chatting and laughter drifted from the living room. Rex appeared at my feet, wagging his tail. Suddenly, I had an idea. If there was a mishap with the cake, I'd be doing everyone a favour. I would avoid the embarrassment that I always felt by my mother; no one would have to eat terrible cake; and Mum would be spared the humiliation of seeing everyone react to her awful cooking.

Without stopping to think it through, I nudged the cheesecake onto the floor. It landed with a splat, right in front of Rex. He didn't react to it; just looked up at me and wagged his tail.

"Go on! It's okay," I whispered. He didn't budge. I guess he knew all about Mum's cooking and even he couldn't be tempted.

I bent down and pushed him gently towards the mess of cheesecake. "It's delicious, try it." The uncooperative little pooch pulled away.

"Sorry, Rex, you have to!" I grabbed his collar and pulled him forcefully to the cheesecake, pushing his face into it. He resisted at first and then happily tucked in.

"Good boy! Good Rex. You're a good little doggy!" He lapped it up and moved into it excitedly.

"No need to get your paws in it." I pulled him back. Unfortunately, he seemed to think I was playing and rolled over, covering himself in chocolate cheesecake.

"No! Bad doggy!" I reached for him and he jumped up at me excitedly. Cheesecake spread from him to me. He jumped around in front of me and I made a futile attempt to extract cheesecake from Santa's beard hanging from my jumper.

"That's enough!" I grabbed at Rex's collar when he dived back into the cheesecake. My fingers slipped with the cheesecake.

"No! No! No!"

Rex ran away from me and onto the beautiful cream rug. I made a dive for him but missed. When I hit the table leg, I groaned and then landed with a thud on the floor.

"No, Rex. Bad dog!" I leapt for him again while he ran around the table. He bumped into the little table with the Christmas tree as he went. The tree fell to the floor, baubles and needles scattering everywhere. Rex seemed to be on a bit of a sugar high. I finally grabbed hold of him but tripped and he yelped as we landed in a heap on the floor.

"Rex!" Mum's high-pitched voice called from the doorway.

"Fire!" Sophie shouted.

"What?"

"The table's on fire!"

She was right; the centrepiece was on fire. I must have knocked the candles over when I fell.

Brian appeared with a wet tea towel and threw it over the table. Everyone stared at me with wide eyes while I looked around to see the lovely dining room covered in chocolate cheesecake and in complete disarray.

"The dog," I said accusingly. "Rex was eating the cheesecake." They looked sceptical. "I just found him eating it. Then he went crazy." I gestured the room.

"Poor Rex," Mum soothed. He looked annoyingly calm and innocent with his big eyes looking up at everyone.

Sophie snorted and started giggling. "You're a disaster!"

"It was the dog," I insisted.

I looked to Brian for support but he was busy patting down the remnants of smouldering leaves on the table.

On reflection, it really hadn't gone to plan. I should've just let them eat the cheesecake.

"Sorry about the cake, Mum."

"Never mind. I'm not sure you would've liked it anyway. My neighbour gave me a strange recipe; it's called Philadelphia cheesecake. It's actually made with Philadelphia cheese spread! Can you believe it? And the base is made from digestive biscuits and golden syrup. Rex probably did us all a favour. I'm sorry about the room though. It's a bit of a mess."

I wiped a blob of the cheesecake from my jumper and stuck it in my mouth. The Philadelphia chocolate cheesecake tasted heavenly. I couldn't help it; I let out a sob and ran past everyone and up the stairs.

Chapter 21

"There's cheesecake in my hair," I said when Brian entered the bathroom after me. "The one time she actually made something normal and I sabotaged it! And I've ruined the dining room."

"I thought it was the dog?"

"Of course it wasn't the bloody dog. It was me. I ruin everything." He smiled and it made me cry. "Don't laugh at me."

"I'm not!" He grinned cheekily and I hit him lightly on the chest. "Honestly," he said trying to control himself. "I'm not laughing at you. But it is quite funny. Look at the state of you."

Holding my shoulders, he turned me toward the mirror. I laughed through my tears. He pulled me back to face him and wrapped his arms around me.

"Brian, I'm covered."

"I don't care." He gave me a big hug and kissed me. "God, this is good cheesecake," he said, licking it from my neck.

I laughed and pushed him away.

"Get in the shower," he said. "I'll try and do something about the dining room."

"I love you," I said, sighing.

"Good! I love you too." He kissed me again. "Now get in the shower."

I glanced at the chocolate smudges down the front of his jumper. "You might need a new top."

"Well, that is a shame." He pulled the door behind him, leaving me to clean myself up.

When I finally forced myself to face everyone downstairs, I glanced into the dining room and found it all cleaned up and missing the lovely cream rug. I followed the sound of laughter into the living room and looked at everyone spread around the room with drinks, and plates with partially eaten slices of Christmas cake on them.

Sophie beckoned me over to sit by her on the floor. She squeezed my arm affectionately. "We're playing charades, if you're wondering why Linda is flapping around like that … oh wait *To Kill a Mockingbird*?"

"Yes," Linda said, delighted.

"My turn." Sophie jumped away from me, into the middle of the room, where Callum handed her a card.

Brian walked into the room with the phone to his ear. "Found her," he said, looking at me.

He handed me the phone.

"Grace?" I asked as I moved towards the quiet of the kitchen. It could only be my best friend, Grace. Everyone else who would call me was already in my living room.

"Happy Christmas!" I said. "I miss you!"

"I miss you, too," she said. "It was a horrible decision to stay in America for Christmas. I wish I was with you. Brian just filled me in and it sounds like you've been having a great time."

"Well apart from me ruining Christmas."

"You're always so dramatic! Brian said you ruined

a cheesecake, he didn't mention anything about you ruining Christmas."

"But I ruined the cheesecake in a very dramatic way." I smiled as the laughter drifted in from the living room. Perhaps I didn't ruin Christmas after all.

"I'm sorry I missed it. We're having lunch with some colleagues and I'm fairly sure there will be nothing as fun as chocolate-covered dogs running wild, upturned Christmas trees and flaming wreaths!"

I had to laugh. "These things always happen to me, don't they? Brian should probably kick me out before I ruin the whole house."

"No way. He loves it." She chuckled. "I booked my flights by the way. I'll be back to visit you in the spring and I need you to help me with my wedding plans. I can't wait. I'll be over for two weeks. Do you think you can take some time off work?"

"Definitely. I can't wait either."

"What about *your* wedding plans?" she said. "Got any ideas yet?"

"Don't you start. Everyone keeps asking me about it." I lowered my voice. "Brian and I even had an argument about it last night."

"What is there to argue about?"

"I don't know. I just feel a bit rushed and pressured. I need some time to decide what I want for my wedding."

"I thought you'd be planning it already. I can't wait to start organising everything. I'm constantly planning mine in my head."

"Yeah, but you've been thinking about it since we were about six. I'm still getting over the shock that someone wants to marry me."

"Don't be daft," she said seriously. "I bet once you help me with my wedding, it'll motivate you. It's all so exciting."

I wasn't so sure. I imagined our ideas about weddings would differ slightly, as did our outlook on most things in life. Our friendship definitely operated under the 'opposites attract' principle.

"I better get back to everyone," I said. "If it's boring with you're colleagues today, just throw some dessert around the place, it'll liven things up!" We said cheerful goodbyes and promised to talk again soon.

As I hung up the phone, I hovered at the edge of the living room for a while, watching everyone. Sophie was standing in the middle of the room pointing at herself while everyone shouted random things at her.

"You can't just tell us it's a film and then point at yourself," Jake complained. "Try doing something else."

"Pretty Woman?" I shouted. I knew Sophie far too well.

"Yes! I thought I'd made it very clear. I don't know why the rest of you couldn't get it."

"Your turn, Marie," Callum called.

"No, that's it for now," Linda said. "It's time for the Queen."

"No!" Callum and Sophie shouted at once.

"You're not seriously going to make us sit through the Queen's speech are you?" Sophie asked.

"Yes, I am. No discussion, I'm afraid. Brian turn the telly on, please."

Linda placated us with a box of Celebrations as we

watched the Queen's speech. Then we set off with another round of charades.

"I better go," Mum said as the afternoon drew on. "I said I'd get Rex back before it got too late."

I shook my head in annoyance at the selfish people who not only farmed their dog off to Mum at every opportunity but also disrupted our Christmas by dictating when she should bring him home.

"I'm going to drive her," Aunt Kath said. "We've got a new DVD to watch this evening. Thanks for a lovely Christmas, Marie."

I waved them off from the front door and hugged myself against the freezing air. A few snowflakes floated on the breeze.

"Well," Brian said as I settled myself next to him in the living room. "Will I ever get my present?"

"Oh! I forgot about it. I'll get it." In the dining room, I hesitantly took the envelope out of the drawer in the dresser.

"Here you go." Nervously, I handed it to him. I could feel everyone watching as he opened it.

"A weekend in The Lake District." He read the printout with false cheer. I knew a weekend away was a boring present.

"Lovely. I love The Lake District," Linda said.

"It's not your only present," I said quickly, desperate to redeem myself. "Hang on …"

I ran upstairs and dragged the big box out of the wardrobe in the spare room. Until then, I'd not been sure if I was going to give him that one. I wasn't sure how he would react to it. I carried it awkwardly back into the living room, wondering if anyone ever got dumped for buying their partner really rubbish presents. Maybe I would be the first.

I placed it on the floor in front of him and his eyes lit up. He tore at the paper and I waited nervously for his reaction.

"Wow!" Callum's voice was full of envy as he ran over to get a closer look.

"You got me Nerf guns?" Brian asked slowly.

"Yes. You can have a whole Nerf war. It's got everything." Brian was staring at me but I couldn't read his expression. It seemed like such a good idea when I was looking at them in the toyshop. I glanced at Sophie who rolled her eyes dramatically.

"Nerf guns?" Brian asked me again, shaking his head slightly. I nodded and grinned like an idiot.

He laughed and started helping Callum open the box. "You're amazing!"

"You like it?" I asked.

"It might be the best present I've ever had." He kissed me before moving back to his new toy.

I looked at Sophie with a smug little smile on my face.

Chapter 22

"I don't want to go," Callum complained a few hours later. There'd been an epic battle of Nerf between him, Brian and Jake. The rest of us kept out of it, apart from getting hit by foam bullets whenever we needed to leave the living room.

We'd watched a few Christmas specials on TV, and brought out a load of sweets and snacks to stuff our faces with. Brian had eventually come back to cuddle up with me in the armchair and everything became more idyllic, the more fizzy wine I drank. I was glad Brian had relaxed and was being his normal self again. He was always so laid back, it had unnerved me to see him so on edge.

"We've got to pick Michael and your gran up from the home," Jake told Callum. "We'll go in for a bit and see all the old dears too. They love it when you visit."

"They'll all pinch my cheeks and tell me I've grown. Can't I sleep here? Please." Callum looked from me to Jake.

"Not tonight. I think Marie and Brian will want some peace. I'm sure they've had enough of us by now."

"Never!" Brian gave Callum a friendly shove and I raised my eyebrows questioningly at Jake. We were getting quite good at this silent communication. I was always worried about saying the wrong thing and telling Callum he could stay when Jake would rather he didn't. Jake shrugged his shoulders in response, giving me the go-ahead.

"It's fine by me," I said to Callum. "If it's okay with Jake."

"Yes! Can I, Jake?"

"Go on then," Jake agreed. "Thanks, Marie."

"It's our pleasure," I told him as Brian high-fived Callum.

"I don't want to go either." Sophie pouted. "It's not fair."

"Get out! Your mum will be waiting for you." I glanced around to check Callum hadn't heard me. Clearly his mum wasn't overly concerned about spending time with him at Christmas. Luckily, he was too busy laughing about something with Brian and Jake. Carol had at least rung to say Happy Christmas to him earlier in the afternoon. Callum seemed to relax after that. I think he was relieved to know that she was okay. As suspected, she'd been out drinking after work and passed out at her boyfriend's house. She was on her way back to work at the bar when she rang Callum.

"I had the best Christmas, Marie." Sophie linked her arm through mine in the hallway.

"I'm glad."

"I mean it." She looked at me sincerely. "It was the best Christmas I've ever had." Her smile spread slowly across her face. "Especially the chocolate dog incident. I can't believe you almost burned the house down!"

I was beginning to see the funny side and smiled when I opened the front door for her.

"Where did that come from?" Sophie said.

We stared, open-mouthed at the crisp, white, blanket of snow over everything. Snow was falling thick and fast, sparkling in front of the street lamp.

"Callum!" we both shouted. I dashed to the hall cupboard and pushed my feet into some boots and pulled a coat and hat on.

"Come on," I said to the others who were moving out of the living room.

I chased Sophie down the steps and into the road, squealing as we went. I'd just picked up a snowball when one hit me on the shoulder.

I looked up at Brian who was standing on the top step trying his best to look innocent. I threw my snowball at him but he dodged it and it hit Linda who was hovering behind him.

"Sorry, Linda!" I shouted.

She brushed at the snow. "You just started a war, young lady!"

"Take cover!" Sophie yelled at me. I followed her to shelter behind a parked car.

"Callum, get over here," she called. "It's young against old."

"Guess I'm on your team," Brian said, following Callum.

"No. You're old!" Callum shouted over his shoulder and aimed a snowball at Brian's head.

Brian quickly retreated when Sophie and I set on him too.

Jake appeared silently from the other side of the car and ran his arm along its roof, spraying snow over all three of us. We were too stunned to get him back and he ran away to take cover.

"I say we make a run for it and attack," Callum whispered. We nodded seriously and took a moment to arm ourselves with snowballs.

"On three," Sophie said. "One, two, three … go!"

We ran screaming around the car and back towards the house, stopping halfway across the road when we realised our enemies were nowhere in sight. I could hear my own heart beating as we looked up and down the deserted road. We stood, silently staring at each other.

I jumped a mile when four car doors opened at once. Linda, George, Jake and Brian piled out of the parked car in front of us, immediately bombarding us with snowballs. We all pelted each other, running up and down the road and between parked cars. It was so much fun.

At least until Linda achieved a direct hit to my face.

I dropped to my knees and wiped blood from the bridge of my nose. "Linda, I think there was a stone it!"

"Everyone stop," she shouted, crouching beside me. "I'm so sorry. Are you okay?"

"Yeah, I can't even feel it, my face is numb from the cold. Game over though. You win!"

Brian appeared and pulled me up, taking my face in his hands to inspect the wound.

"It's fine," I said.

"Why are you crying then? Does is need stitching?"

"I'm not crying. My eyes are just watering from

154

the cold. I'm not having stitches on my nose. Anyway it's only a scratch, stop fussing." Everyone huddled around me. "Let's not stop having fun just because Linda almost knocked me out!" I said.

"Can we build snowmen?" Callum asked.

"Yes." I shooed everyone away from me. "Great idea."

Linda handed me a tissue and I pressed it to my nose. "I really am sorry," she said.

"It's fine," I insisted.

Linking my arm through Brian's, we walked to where the others were rolling snowballs into snowmen.

Brian moved away to help Callum lift the head onto his snowman. When he came back to me, I rested my head on his shoulder. We watched as a variety of snowmen were created in front of our house. I finally gave in when my feet started to go numb, and suggested we move back into the warmth.

"I've got to go," Jake said. "I'm going to be in trouble with Michael. I was supposed to be there ages ago. Want a lift, Sophie?"

"Yes, please." She hugged me again before moving towards Jake's car. Luckily we'd cleared most of the snow from the car during our snowball fight so it wasn't much effort to clear the remaining bits.

Linda and George left too. Brian, Callum and I stood on the top step waving as the cars crawled slowly down the snowy street.

"Get your pyjamas on, Callum." I rubbed my freezing hands together. "We'll have hot chocolate by the fire." He ran upstairs. Sometimes he ended up staying with us after our games nights so he always had a pair of pyjamas in the spare room.

"I'm going to get my pyjamas on too." I gave Brian a quick kiss. "I'm freezing!"

"I guess I'm making hot chocolate?" he called after me as I hurried up the stairs.

"Good guess!"

Chapter 23

"That was the best Christmas I've ever had." I snuggled up to Brian when we finally climbed into bed. It had been a long day. After being adamant I wanted my first Christmas with Brian to be a quiet one, I was so glad we'd ended up with our friends and family around us.

"It was fun," Brian said, pulling the covers over us.

"It was perfect." I smiled and ran a hand down his cheek. "Apart from the cheesecake."

He chuckled. "Apart from that."

"I hope we're always this happy," I said as my eyelids got heavier.

Brian turned on his side to look at me. "You are happy then?"

I frowned and stroked his hair. My drunken comments about not wanting a wedding had obviously got him worried. "Of course I'm happy. I really do want to marry you. It's the wedding that freaks me out not being married. If we could wake up tomorrow married I'd be ecstatic."

"I just don't really understand why you don't want a wedding. It's only a party. And surely getting married is something to celebrate."

I nodded and looked at him intensely. He was right. I wasn't even sure myself why the thought of a wedding terrified me so much.

"Sophie said they do wedding packages at the hotel where she works," I said vaguely. "So that's an option, I suppose."

Brian smiled. "You don't sound enthusiastic."

"I'm not. I honestly don't know what I want to do though."

"But we can cross off getting married in a hotel? That's a start."

"I suppose." I sighed. "Was it just the wedding that was bothering you?"

He shifted onto his back and his gaze moved to the ceiling. "Yes."

"Really?"

He frowned but didn't look at me.

"Tell me if there's something else going on," I said.

"Maybe I was worrying about nothing," he said vaguely.

"What do you mean?" I propped my chin on his chest and he wrapped his arms around my back.

"Do you think I work too much?"

"Not really," I said. "Why?"

He chewed on his bottom lip. "I'm always home later than you. Sometimes I come home really late, and I worry that you're always hanging around waiting for me."

I grinned. "As long as there's wine in the fridge I'm quite happy waiting for you!"

He gently rubbed my back. "I just want you to be happy," he said. "I was worried for a while that you weren't."

I stared at him, surprised that he'd ever question

whether I was happy with him.

"I've never been happier," I said seriously. "I have everything I ever wanted."

"And you'd tell me if you weren't happy?"

"Yes. I love our life. I worry that your work stresses you out, but it doesn't bother me if you have to work late."

"Okay." He ran a hand over my hair.

"I'll think some more about the wedding," I said. "I definitely want us to be married by next Christmas."

"That sounds great." He smiled and shuffled to get comfy on the pillow.

Brian fell asleep quickly, and I ended up tossing and turning. My mind was racing and it took me a long time to fall asleep.

I was awake again before I knew it. It was rare that I was awake before Brian so I productively took the opportunity to stare at his sleeping form. Sunlight gradually seeped through the curtains casting a warm glow on the room.

"Don't watch me sleep, it's creepy." Brian's gravelly voice made me jump.

"I was thinking about the wedding." I decided not to question how he knew I was watching him even though his eyes were firmly closed.

He rolled onto his side. "Had any bright ideas?"

"Actually, yes. I was thinking we could go away somewhere to get married, just the two of us?"

His eyebrows knitted together. "Sophie, for one, would never forgive you."

"She'd get over it. I just think it would be so much easier if we go away and get married. Then it's done and everyone will stop asking about it."

He propped himself up on an elbow. "Very romantic."

"It came out wrong," I said, screwing my nose up. "I just don't want a big fuss. And I don't want to have to worry about offending my mum by telling her she can't make my dress, and that I don't want Rex to be part of the ceremony."

Brian smiled. "Okay. I understand you don't want your mum having much of a say in things. But eloping seems a bit drastic. Couldn't we do something a little bit more traditional?" He pushed my hair back behind my ear and looked at me with his gorgeous brown eyes.

I felt a lump in my throat. It had hit me at some point in the night - the real reason I was avoiding any mention of a wedding - and then I couldn't fall back to sleep for thinking about it.

"I can't." My voice came out as a croak. Brian moved his hand to mine and waited for me to continue. "Traditionally my parents would pay for the wedding–" he tried to interrupt but I put a hand to his lips.

"And my father would give me away. My mum would help me choose a dress and find a venue and help with choosing flowers and all the little details that my mum just isn't capable of. Every time I think about these perfect fairy tale weddings I know there are so many reasons why I won't ever get that. So, I do want to marry you, but I just want to do it quietly and without any fuss." I kissed him lightly on the lips. "Okay?"

When he didn't say anything, I got out of bed and

put my dressing gown on.

Brian sat up and pulled me back on to the bed next to him. "You can have a perfect wedding. It might not be anything from a fairy tale but it will be perfect for us. We can do whatever we want." I felt a little better as he hugged me and planted a kiss on my forehead. "And stop worrying about money."

I rolled my eyes and stood up again. "Says the man who's got loads."

"Says the woman who's marrying him!" He grinned cheekily and I couldn't help but smile as I moved out of the bedroom to follow the sound of Callum's laughter.

Down in the kitchen, Callum and Sophie looked up from a game of cards.

"What are you doing here?" I asked.

"What a lovely welcome," Sophie said. "Thanks!"

"I didn't say you weren't welcome. I just wondered what we'd done to deserve the pleasure of your company again so soon."

"I was just thinking of Callum having to put up with you two old farts on his own. I thought I'd come and keep him company. Plus, my mum's house is a nightmare. The crazy woman should really have thought about space at some point rather than just popping out more kids. You can hardly move without falling over a small child."

I looked at her sympathetically. Although she joked a lot, she never really complained. It must be hard for her. She didn't earn enough money to be able to move out.

The four of us had a lazy breakfast of toast and tea and I didn't bother getting dressed until late in the morning. Jake and Michael arrived to pick Callum up but he was halfway through one of the *Star Wars* films, so they joined him and Brian in front of the TV.

Linda was the next to arrive. I'd stop being surprised by random visitors at my door a while ago.

She looked apologetic as she stepped inside. "I know this is quite cheeky but I realised that since we had Christmas dinner with you, we didn't have any leftovers … and it really wouldn't be Boxing Day without leftovers, would it? I know you had a lot so I thought you wouldn't mind if I came and grabbed a bit."

I smiled at her. "Of course. Everyone is here. We can all have lunch together. I think we'll just be eating from our knees though. The boys are engrossed in the TV. Where's George?"

"He wasn't feeling great. Probably just a bit worn out after all the excitement yesterday." That was Linda's polite way of saying he'd had enough of us yesterday.

She hung up her coat and shouted hello to everyone in the living room. "I wanted to talk to you about something as well, Marie."

I was intrigued as she followed me into the kitchen. While she took a seat, I flicked the switch on the kettle.

"I wanted to talk to you about the wedding."

"We really don't know what we're going to do yet," I said.

"Yes. I know that," she said firmly. "Just let me talk for once!"

I kept quiet and took a seat on the stool next to her.

"All I wanted to say is that I would really like to

help you with anything you need." I was about to jump in, but I saw her eyes start to well up so I just put my hand on her arm and stayed quiet.

"You know I'm very fond of you?" She looked at me seriously and I nodded. "I think of you as family and as I don't have children, there's some things I feel I'm missing out on. I always thought it would be lovely to have a daughter to go shopping with and go out to lunch with ..." My eyes filled with tears as Linda fished in her handbag for a tissue to dry her eyes with.

"Sorry." She sniffed. "I didn't think I'd get so emotional. I had this little speech planned. Anyway, it's been so lovely getting to do all those things with you and I just wanted you to know that whatever you decide about the wedding, it would mean a lot to me to help you with any plans. But I don't want you to feel any pressure and I know you've got your mum to help you ..."

"I'd love it if you helped me." I reached over to steal a tissue from her. I could hardly speak for the lump in my throat.

"There's one more thing," she said. "I spoke to George, and he agreed, so you can't say no. I want to pay for your dress; whatever you want. Don't say no! It's just something that I want to do for you."

I could no longer see for tears, and when she wrapped her arms around me I felt all the tension leave my body and I sobbed into her shoulder.

"Is that okay?" she asked.

"Yes. Thank you," I managed to quietly whisper into her shoulder.

"Marie?" Brian's voice interrupted us and I pulled

away from Linda and wiped at my snotty, tear-covered face.

"What's wrong?" Worry was etched in his features as he came and put his arms around me. So much for me convincing him I was happy; now I was crying my eyes out in the kitchen.

"I'm fine," I said, spluttering a laugh. "They're happy tears."

He wiped my cheeks with his thumbs. "What are you so happy about then?"

"Wedding planning, if you can believe that! Can you send Sophie in here?"

As Brian walked out of the kitchen, I moved to open a drawer and dig out a pen and notebook.

"What's going on?" Sophie asked.

"We've got some wedding planning to do." I passed the notebook to Linda. Then I looked back at Sophie.

"What?" she asked as I stared at her.

"Will you be my bridesmaid?"

The smile spread slowly across her face before she flung her arms around me. "Yes! Of course."

"Right then ..." I went back to the stool beside Linda. Sophie hopped up to sit on the counter. "I'll need to decide on a venue," I said. "Linda's taking me shopping for a dress ..."

Sophie grinned. "I was looking forward to seeing you in one of your mum's creations for the big day."

I laughed and shook my head. "What else needs to go on the list, Linda?"

"Well there's flowers, caterers, cake, cars ..." She scribbled as she spoke and I got dizzier the longer the list got.

"This seems like a lot," I said.

"Sorry. I'm getting carried away. I'm just brainstorming. You might not want all this but it's things to think about."

Brian stuck his head around the door. "Everything okay, ladies?"

"Fine!" I said with a grin. "Linda might be about to bankrupt us though."

His eyes twinkled when he smiled at me. "It better be a good party then."

I beamed back at him. "It's going to be amazing!"

Chapter 24

I didn't know wedding planning could be so much fun. I spent the afternoon chatting and laughing with Sophie and Linda. Sophie had some wild ideas about the hen night. I indulged her and we had a good giggle about it, but at some point I'd have to tell her it would need to be a slightly tamer affair. After all, the guest list would include such innocents as my mum, Linda and Anne.

The afternoon whizzed by; the boys joined us in the kitchen and we ate leftovers from Christmas dinner. The atmosphere was relaxed and cheerful. It was hard to believe that not so long ago I didn't know these people at all. I couldn't imagine my life without them now.

The house felt eerily quiet once they'd all left. Brian and I sat alone on the couch. The lights glowed on the Christmas tree making the room wonderfully cosy.

I sat crossed-legged on the couch, glancing through the notes Linda had made in my little wedding notebook.

"I might turn into one of those really annoying people who can only talk about their wedding. You're completely right about choosing a wedding that suits us. There are so many options. You can get married in a theme park or in a stately home …"

He chuckled and lay back, lifting his feet into my lap. "Weren't you worried about your mum's wacky ideas?"

"Yes, but that's when I thought we had to do the traditional white wedding. If we get married in a barn or on a beach, it won't be so weird having the dog carry the rings …" I tapped the pen against my bottom lip. "Although, I found a place on the internet that has owls that fly in with the rings. How amazing would that be?"

"Totally amazing," he said mockingly.

"I'm just excited to have options. Everyone kept talking as though we'd do something really traditional and it didn't appeal at all."

Brian's grin spread slowly over his face. "You know all the times you roll your eyes at you mum, and say she's quirky and eccentric …?"

I shoved his feet off me and crawled on top of him, laughing. "I'm nothing like my mother!"

"You just keep telling yourself that."

I dug him in the ribs until he pushed my hand away, laughing loudly. "I take it back! You're nothing like your mother. She wants the rings brought in on the back of a dog and you want them on the back of an owl. That's not alike at all!"

"I kind of presumed the owl would carry them in its beak," I said flatly. "If they're on its back I don't think I'm that bothered."

"I don't want my ring in an owls mouth."

"Fine. Rex gets to carry the rings then!"

"Just don't let him near the wedding cake," Brian said with a twinkle in his eyes.

I kissed his lips. "You should take time off work more often. I didn't like it when you were so stressed out."

"Me neither." He sighed and tucked my hair behind my ear. "We'll also have a honeymoon to look forward to soon."

"I didn't even think about that. There's so much to organise."

"I know a good travel agent," he said. "Arranging the honeymoon should be a breeze."

"Yes." I grinned. "I can do it on work time!"

"I was referring to Anne," he said. "You can book holidays too, can you?"

"You're so cheeky today!" I tickled his ribs again and didn't stop until he'd gone bright red from laughing.

Chapter 25

With Brian in such a good mood, I decided to cancel my Saturday morning shopping with Linda and spend the day with him instead. I wasn't actually sure we were definitely on for shopping, what with it being so soon after Christmas, but Linda really was a creature of habit so I thought it best to send a quick message so she didn't arrive on the doorstep.

I slid the phone onto the counter when Brian wandered into the kitchen, fresh from the shower. I was still in my pyjamas.

"Shall we have a day out somewhere?" I asked.

"Yes. What do you have in mind?"

"How about we drive out into the countryside, and have a nice walk? We could find a country pub for lunch."

"There's always a pub when you makes plans, isn't there?"

I laughed. "What's your suggestion then?"

"I was thinking a walk and pub lunch!"

"Funny that," I said grinning.

"Great minds think alike." He leaned over and kissed me. "You might need more clothes on. It's chilly out."

I screwed my nose up. "These are my winter pyjamas. With a coat they'll be fine, won't they?" I slid off the stool, laughing.

"I dare you!"

"You shouldn't dare me. You'll be the one embarrassed when you're sitting in the pub with me in my pyjamas."

"That's true. Maybe you should get dressed."

"I'll hop in the shower quickly."

When I went to pass him, he snaked an arm around my waist and pulled me to him.

"What are you doing?" I asked happily.

"Kissing you," he mumbled as he nuzzled my neck. He dotted kisses along my jaw before finally reaching my lips.

"I love you," he said when we finally broke apart.

"I love you too." Squeezing him tight, I inhaled his wonderfully fresh scent. I was fairly sure I didn't smell anywhere near as good. A shower was definitely needed. "I'll get ready quickly," I said and pecked him on the lips before hurrying upstairs.

I was happy about the prospect of a day out with Brian. It hardly took me anytime to get showered and dressed. Then I rushed back downstairs again.

"What's happened?" My stomach lurched when I walked into the kitchen.

I'd never seen Brian looking so grave. He was sitting on a barstool with his head propped up on his hand, looking absolutely miserable. Everything had been perfect quarter of an hour ago. What on earth had happened?

"You're worrying me." I went and put a hand on his shoulder. "What's going on?"

My phone was lying on the counter in front of him and he pushed it towards me. "You had a message from Jason."

The mention of Jason made me slightly nauseous. No wonder Brian looked so glum. That's pretty much how I felt whenever Jason messaged me too.

Groaning, I reached for the phone. "What does *he* want?" I brought up the message.

Let me know when Brian's out and I'll nip round. It's about time we worked up a sweat together again x

I smiled. Even though I hated the exercising, he was quite entertaining.

My smile slipped when I caught Brian watching me intently. It only then occurred to me that he had no idea who Jason was. I read the message again. Then looked back at Brian.

"That's absolutely not how it sounds …" I laughed nervously. "I mean, you don't think …"

Brian continued to stare at me. My mind whirred. Surely he didn't think I was cheating on him. The idea was so ridiculous I struggled to wrap my head around it.

I shook my head. "That's really not how it seems."

Brian leaned forward and pushed his hands through his hair.

Tears stung my eyes. "Please don't tell me you think I'm seeing someone else?"

"Well, aren't you?"

"No!" I didn't know whether to laugh or cry. It was completely insane. "Of course not."

"Then how the hell do you explain that message?"

"I can't believe you think I'd cheat on you." I picked up the phone and read Jason's message again. Okay, it was fairly incriminating but I still couldn't quite grasp the idea that Brian could ever think I was cheating on him. I was torn between explaining myself and shouting at him for his lack of trust.

I took a deep breath and slipped onto the stool beside Brian. "Jason's a personal trainer."

He turned his head and stared at me.

"He is." I frowned and bit my lip. "Of course I'm not cheating on you. I would never cheat on you. How can you think that?"

"I don't know what to think."

"Honestly, Jason is a fitness instructor. I met him through work and I was having some personal training sessions with him. I told him I was giving it up over Christmas and he keeps messaging me. He's way more concerned about my health than I am!"

"It's not just that message." Brian fiddled with his watch strap. "A while ago I came home from work early–"

"Oh my god! You noticed the two water glasses? You're like a detective."

Brian's forehead wrinkled in a frown. "Your phone was on the counter and a message flashed up. Something about a close call and he didn't appreciate being pushed out of the back door. What water glasses?"

"Never mind."

"When I came home early, you shoved a guy out the backdoor and then ran upstairs for a shower."

I grimaced. "That seems bad."

"He's a fitness instructor?" he asked slowly.

I chewed on my thumbnail and nodded.

"You're not sleeping with him?"

Tears filled my eyes and rolled slowly down my

cheeks. "Of course I'm not sleeping with him."

For a moment, we sat in silence. I was heartbroken Brian could think I'd cheat on him. And furious with him too. But I was also really upset that he'd clearly spent weeks wondering if I was seeing someone else. No wonder he'd been in such a foul mood.

"Why didn't you say something?" I asked quietly, tears still falling silently down my cheeks.

"I don't know. I didn't want it to be true. I kept telling myself it *couldn't* be true." He sighed. "I was terrified of losing you."

"You idiot." I leaned over and rested my head on his shoulder. "All the times I told you I loved you – did you think I was lying?"

"I honestly didn't know what to think." He took my hand and pulled it to his lips to kiss my fingers. "I'm sorry."

"I would never do that," I said adamantly. We'd both been cheated on in the past and I would never do that to anyone. "And why would I, when I've got you?"

He turned to face me. "I don't understand why you didn't tell me you had a personal trainer."

"It's embarrassing! And I thought you'd have an issue with it."

"Why would I have an issue with it? And why is it embarrassing?"

"If you saw me running through the streets and flinging myself about in the park, you wouldn't ask why it's embarrassing!"

He started laughing and the tension left his shoulders. "I can't believe you didn't tell me."

"It was after that work party. I was worried you'd

think I was being insecure after seeing all the skinny tarts you work with. Except they're not skinny tarts." I rolled my eyes. "They're beautiful, intelligent women."

Brian opened his mouth but I just spoke louder. "I know what you're going to say: that you love me for my sparkling personality and you don't care how I look. That's why I didn't tell you about Jason. I'm not doing it to get skinny and beautiful." I raised an eyebrow. "Jason's no miracle worker."

"That's not what I was going to say," he said with a hint of a smile.

I put a finger on his lips to silence him. "I just want to be a bit healthier that's all." I paused. "Why are you smirking?"

"The sparkling personality comment."

"What's funny about that?"

"You realise your personality is much more of an acquired taste than your looks?"

I hopped off the stool and slapped him playfully on the chest. He pulled me into him and kissed me.

"I love how you look," he murmured. "And I love your wacky personality, but if you want to do some exercise I'm not going to say anything."

"I'm not sure I *want* to. But Jason comes in the shop a lot and nags me. And since I started jogging I set myself some goals so I thought it would be good to keep at it."

"You're not going to run a marathon are you?"

I laughed. "No. My aim is to be able to run and have a conversation at the same time. A marathon is probably a little too ambitious."

He pressed his forehead against mine and looked

at me seriously. "I'm sorry I jumped to conclusions."

"I'm sorry you did too. Don't do that again."

He hugged me tighter. "I'm so relieved."

"Shall we still go out for our pub lunch?"

"Yes." He bit his lip and glanced at my phone. "There's just one problem … I might have accidentally replied to Jason's message."

My eyes widened and I grabbed at the phone. Previously, I'd only been concentrating on Jason's message, but when I looked below it there was a message which *I'd* apparently sent in reply.

"Oh, no." I dropped my head to Brian's shoulder. "You've no idea what you've done."

Chapter 26

I held the phone up to Brian in disbelief. The message simply read *I'm free now. Come over.*

"You told him to come here?" I screeched. "What were you thinking?"

"I was thinking that if you were seeing someone else, I wanted to know who he was."

I tutted and shook my head at him, all previous emotions replaced by the fear of imminent exercise. "I can't believe you invited him over? What have you done?"

"What have *I* done? You're the one with a secret personal trainer."

"It's Christmas," I whined, ignoring the comment. Yes, it was ridiculous that I had a secret personal trainer but I didn't have time to dwell on that. "I want to go to the pub, not do exercise!"

"Just tell him that."

"You don't know what he's like. He won't take no for an answer. I cannot believe you replied to his message. I'm going to have to go jogging now. It's cold. I don't want to go running with the flipping energiser bunny."

"Message him again and say you've changed your mind."

"He'll already be on his way. And he'll charge me

for the session now whatever. He's mean like that. This is all your fault. You may as well get changed because if I have to go jogging, I'm taking you with me."

Brian shook his head. "No chance. Besides, none of this is my fault. If you didn't have your phone set to show messages on a locked screen I'd never have read your messages."

I rolled my eyes and smiled at him.

"Why do you look so amused?" he asked.

"I was just thinking it's a little bit crazy of you to message Jason. What were you thinking you'd do, have a punch up over me?"

"I didn't think it through." He rested his hands on my hips and smiled sheepishly.

I nodded. "It was really quite irrational and impulsive."

"What's your point?"

"It just seems like you're not so perfect after all. Nice to know I'm not the only crazy one around here!"

He gave me a playful nudge.

"Anyway, you've ruined our day now," I said. "Go and get changed, he'll be here soon."

"I'm not going jogging," Brian said, laughing.

"Yes, you are. You've brought this on yourself. It's terrible by the way. Jason is basically a bully and it's horrible. And did I mention we have to pay for this torture?"

"We're not going jogging!"

"We won't be safe anymore," I mused. "He could turn up at any moment in his skimpy little shorts and force us into sit ups, squats and star jumps."

I was interrupted by a knock at the front door.

"This is it, Brian. Life as we know it is over!" I grinned at him and headed for the door.

Brian followed. "I'll just tell him to go. This is crazy."

"No." I switched to a whisper while we moved down the hall. "You can't just tell him. He'll talk you into a workout. Just let me speak to him, I can lie my way out of this like I always do …"

I didn't wait for Brian to respond, just shoved him behind the door while I opened it a fraction and stuck my head out to Jason. He was jogging on the spot.

"Come on then?" he said, grinning at me.

"Jason, it's thick snow!"

He stopped and looked around, as though he hadn't even noticed. "It's just a sprinkling." There was something seriously wrong with him. In my book, jogging was not an all-weather activity.

"Sorry." I switched to a stage whisper. "Brian came home unexpectedly. I can't come for a workout after all."

"Why don't you just tell him? This is a bad time of year. You need to keep active and not sit at home in front of the TV feeding your face with junk."

"We talked about this. It's called Christmas. That's what normal people do. Let's just wait until the New Year and then I'll tell Brian and I'll be yours to torment. We can even drag Brian out with us too!"

I felt Brian gently dig me in the ribs but my suggestion seemed to placate Jason, who resumed running on the spot. "Fine. You're off the hook until next week." He headed down the steps before turning to look back at me. "I'm charging you full price for today though."

"Whatever!" I grinned at him and closed the door.

Brian smiled at me. "You're not getting me jogging."

"We'll see!" I leaned into him. "I can't believe you thought I'd cheat on you."

He grimaced. "I'm sorry. I'll make it up to you."

"Yes. You will." I nodded and stroked his cheek as I kissed him deeply. His arms tightened around my waist. "I don't really feel like going out anymore," I murmured into his lips.

"What do you want to do?" he said between eager kisses.

"I thought you might have some ideas of how you're going to make it up to me …"

His lips trailed over the skin of my neck and my jaw. When he finally looked at me, his eyes sparkled with mischief. "I've got lots of ideas."

Chapter 27

The next few days went by in a happy blur. Brian and I reverted to the honeymoon stage of our relationship where we just couldn't get enough of each other. We kept to ourselves and basked in our own happy little bubble.

By Monday, we decided fresh air might do us good and ventured out for our walk in the countryside and a pub lunch. Other than that, we barely left the house between Christmas and New Year. It all felt pretty perfect.

We had a very brief discussion about going out on New Year's Eve but quickly dismissed it in favour of staying in and eating frozen pizza and the remainder of the Christmas chocolates. I was cosy in my pyjamas by seven o'clock. When the knock came at the front door, I didn't think much of it at all.

Sophie, Linda and Jake stood on the doorstep.

"What are you doing?" I poked my tooth with my tongue where I'd got a piece of toffee stuck.

"Fat club," Sophie said. "You did say we were meeting at your place now and not Grace's. We listened to you for once."

"It's Wednesday today," I said.

"I'm fairly sure it's Thursday actually," Sophie said.

"It Thursday," Jake agreed.

"Yes." Linda nodded. "Thursday today."

I put a hand on my hip and glared at Sophie. "I spoke to you yesterday and told you I was having a quiet New Years Eve with Brian."

"How was it?" she asked flatly.

"It hasn't happened yet because it's only Wednesday."

Sophie sighed. "I was sure it was Thursday today."

I laughed as Brian arrived behind me and slung and arm over my shoulder. "Evening everyone."

They all said hello and smiled sweetly.

"They're trying to convince me it's fat club today," I told him. There was a clinking sound coming from the bag in Jake's hand. "What's in there?" I asked.

"Champagne," he said proudly.

"You were bringing champagne to fat club?"

"Yep! To celebrate the first fat club of the year and the brand new location."

"It's only Wednesday," I said with a laugh.

Sophie shook her head. "I could've sworn it was Thursday. Is it okay if we come in and wait?"

"Wait for what?"

"Thursday!" they said in unison.

I opened the door wider. I should really have guessed they'd turn up. Sophie messaging to ask what our plans were for New Year's Eve should have been a clue.

"I was planning on lying on the couch all evening, kissing Brian," I said to Sophie as they all moved inside. "You've ruined that plan."

"Yeah, you shouldn't do that," she replied. "Not

with kids in the house. It would be slightly inappropriate."

"I'd hardly call you lot kids."

She grinned, then turned back and cupped her hand over her mouth. "Callum! You can come out now."

I chuckled as Callum crept out from behind the bush, closely followed by Michael, George and Jeff.

I looked questioningly at Sophie.

"We got back together," she said with a grin.

"Good." I gave her a big hug and followed everyone into the living room. Jake and Michael got to work pouring drinks and we were soon merrily sitting around chatting and laughing.

When my glass was almost empty, I wandered into the kitchen to find another bottle of wine. Brian followed me in.

"Did you know they were coming?" he asked quietly.

"I know I'm pretty casual, Brian, but if I'd known they were coming, I wouldn't have put my pyjamas on at six o'clock!"

"It's hard to know with you. You keep odd secrets from me."

"Oh, shut up!"

We were grinning at each other when Sophie wandered in. She hopped up to sit on the counter with a glass of wine in her hand.

"I've had an amazing idea for your wedding," she said.

"What?" I asked.

"You should elope."

"Funnily enough, I did consider that. Brian said you'd never forgive me."

"You could take me with you." She took a sip of her drink. "I'm sick of winter. We could jet off somewhere next week. Get a bit of sun. Sit on a beach drinking cocktails." She waved the wine glass in her hand. "You can get married. It'd be great. You'd need to pay for me since I'm a bridesmaid but I can't imagine that would be a problem." Her eyes roamed the kitchen pointedly. To be fair, it was a bit fancy.

Callum called to Sophie from the living room and she hopped off the counter. "Think about it," she said before leaving us alone again.

"Not the worst idea," Brian said.

"Don't be ridiculous. She's only after a free holiday!"

"Probably. I still like the sound of it."

I took the bottle of wine from the fridge door and filled my glass. "There's no way we can elope. I spent all that time wedding planning with Linda. And she's adamant she's buying my dress."

"I don't mean jet off next week without telling anyone. I mean get married on a beach somewhere hot." He nodded in the direction of the living room. "Take that lot with us."

"Are you serious?"

"Imagine all of us chilling out on the beach every day. In the evenings we can drink cocktails and watch the sun go down …"

"Fat club holiday! It does sound fun." The more I thought about it, the more it seemed like a great idea. I loved the thought of us all together at some fancy resort, relaxing and having fun. "I'm kind of tempted."

"Me too," he said. "We'll have to wait a while

though before we bring it up. I don't want Sophie thinking it's all her idea."

"Good point. We'd never hear the end of it."

"We can wait a few weeks and then pass it off as my idea."

I shook my head. "I'll say it's *my* idea."

"No way anyone would believe you'd come up with such a brilliant idea. I'm the brains of this outfit, you're the quirky personality!"

I pulled a face at him.

"And the insane good looks," he added cheekily.

"Yes, don't forget that." I draped my arms around his neck. "It's a good idea though."

"It's a *great* idea."

I grinned, happy that our crazy friends had gate-crashed yet again. It was lovely to hear the laughter drifting from the living room. "I feel like we're in for a really fun year," I said.

He kissed me lightly on the lips. "I can't wait."

THE END

Acknowledgements

Thanks so much to my amazing team.
Sandra Ellis, Stephen Ellis, Mario Ellis, Emma
Lenze, Meghan Driscoll, Emma-Jane Hannah,
Anthea Kirk and Dua Roberts.
I couldn't do it without you

Other books by Hannah Ellis.

Friends Like These
My Kind of Perfect (Friends Like These book 3)

The Cottage at Hope Cove (Hope Cove book 1)
Escape to Oakbrook Farm (Hope Cove book 2)
Summer at the Old Boathouse (Hope Cove book 3)
Whispers at the Bluebell Inn (Hope Cove book 4)
The House on Lavender Lane (Hope Cove book 5) – coming
Spring 2019

Always With You

Beyond the Lens (Lucy Mitchell Book 1)
Beneath These Stars (Lucy Mitchell Book 2)

A note from the author

Dear Reader,

Thanks so much for choosing to read Christmas with Friends. If you enjoyed it, please take a moment to write an Amazon review. A couple of sentences would be really helpful.

I love to interact with readers, so please feel free to get in touch:

Find me on Facebook: @novelisthannahellis

Follow me on Twitter: @BooksEllis

Read on for a sample of the next book in the series, 'My Kind of Perfect' …

MY KIND OF PERFECT

(FRIENDS LIKE THESE BOOK 3)

HANNAH ELLIS

Chapter 1

I wasn't particularly surprised when I walked into work to find my middle-aged colleague, Anne, dancing around the room with my accidental personal trainer, Jason.

"You realise this is a Thursday morning in a travel agency and not a Saturday night in a club?" I had to speak loudly to make myself heard over the sound of Beyoncé blaring out of a pair of portable speakers lying on Anne's desk.

I dropped into my office chair and shoved my bag into the cabinet by my feet. Jason and Anne were really throwing themselves into the dance moves. Thankfully, the window was almost completely covered by posters and holiday adverts so passers-by couldn't see in.

Anne beckoned me over with a wave of the hand. "Come and join in."

"What are you doing?" I asked.

"I read an article about productivity in the workplace," Jason said, still bopping around the place. "It claimed that starting the day with music and dancing improves staff motivation which leads to increased productivity. It creates a happier workforce, which is good for everyone. Greg agreed I could test the theory on you two."

Greg was the boss in our little shop. There were just the three of us - Greg, Anne and me. We'd been working together for years and balanced each other well. It was always a relaxed atmosphere in our little travel agency.

"Anne's always happy," I pointed out. It was an annoying trait as far as I was concerned. She was constantly chirpy, even first thing in the morning. It baffled me, but I'd grown used to it.

"That's why *you* need to get up and dance!" Anne said.

"Oh! So this is all for my benefit, is it?"

"Mostly, yeah." Jason threw his arms up in the air and spun around, showing off his ridiculous clothing ensemble. This morning he'd opted for yellow shorts (very yellow and very short) with a tight orange T-shirt and leg warmers. The rest of him could freeze but apparently he needed his calves to be well wrapped up. He'd just managed to tie his silky blonde locks back into a ponytail, albeit with strands falling forward over his bright blue eyes.

"Well, I won't be dancing at work." I managed to keep a straight face as I watched Jason shimmy up to Anne with some dirty dancing moves. "It's very unprofessional if you ask me."

"Told you," Anne said.

"Told him what?" I asked, with the distinct feeling that I was walking into a trap.

"I said there's no way you'd dance. I know you so well. It's okay! Some people aren't as good at letting go as others."

Jason winked at me. "I said I bet you had some moves."

"I do, as it happens."

"Prove it," he challenged. The song ended, and as the

next song kicked in, I reluctantly rose from my chair and began an awkward dance toward the middle of the room. Anne gave a little cheer and moved towards me, shaking her shoulders so her sizeable bosom bounced in front of her. I did a twirl in order to move away from her, and laughed at how ridiculous my morning was. I relaxed and found myself getting lost in the music, suddenly not caring that I looked like an absolute lunatic. I let myself go and it could easily have been a Saturday night on a sticky dance floor somewhere.

Getting carried away, I stepped onto the chair and then my desk. Technically, Anne and I shared a desk. It was one long table, which curved down the length of the room like a wave. Anne and Jason cheered me on and I danced my heart out, strutting my stuff along the entire length of the desk.

I was flinging my arms around wildly when I noticed Greg standing in his office doorway, watching me. His arms were folded against his chest and one eyebrow was slightly raised. Greg was a serious sort of guy but he was also a big softie. I knew I wouldn't be in any trouble, but he could definitely put an end to the fun with just a look.

Jason moved to stop the music as Greg's presence killed the atmosphere. I was left feeling slightly awkward as I stood on the desk looking down.

Greg's stern expression didn't change as he held out his hand with a five-pound note in it. Jason took it from him, then turned to high five Anne.

"He didn't think I could get you to dance," Jason told me with a grin.

Greg remained unsmiling as he looked up at me. "I

argued you were far too professional to dance at work."

"It's because I'm so dedicated that I did it!" I protested. "I was totally against the idea but Jason told me about the article about increased productivity …" I glared at Jason as I stepped down from the desk. "You made all that up, didn't you?"

I went back to my chair as he and Anne collapsed into fits of giggles.

"I only did it to improve productivity," I said again.

"So you think you could be more productive?" Greg asked.

"No! Of course not … but …" I realised I was digging myself a hole so I stopped talking and turned on my computer. "See, I've got work to do. I'm not standing around giggling like some people." I glared at Anne. The corners of Greg's mouth twitched to a smile before he disappeared into his office at the back of the shop.

"You were right," Jason said to me. "You do have some moves!" He snorted as he re-enacted some of my dance moves, making Anne even more hysterical.

"Don't you have a job to get to?" I asked him. Jason was a regular visitor to our shop. He'd jogged in one day to book a holiday. He and Anne had hit it off and he kept coming back as though it was some sort of social club.

Somehow, he'd also talked me into some personal training sessions. Initially I'd hated every second of our workouts but they'd grown on me, mainly because Jason was such a sweet guy and a lot of fun to be around. His impromptu visits to the shop were always well received. He'd sit and drink coffee with us as he gossiped about his clients and told us stories.

He groaned as he moved to the door. "I've got a session with Little Miss Chihuahua. I'll be back later with stories no doubt." Jason had a strict code of confidentiality when it came to his clients. He wouldn't use their real names but had nicknames for them all. He'd hinted that we'd know Little Miss Chihuahua, who insisted on bringing her tiny dog to her workout sessions. He claimed to have a few celebrity clients, although there was a good chance Anne and I would never have heard of them even if he did name them.

"See you after work," he called to me as he headed for the door.

"We can skip today if you're too busy, I don't mind!" I was trying my luck and we both knew it.

He laughed as he waved back at us and took off running up the road.

"He's a funny one, isn't he?" Anne chuckled as she made for the coffee machine in the corner of the room. "He really brightens the place up."

"Greg and I not good enough for you?" I asked.

"Oh you're all right, I suppose." She grinned as she handed me a coffee. "Have you got anything nice planned for the weekend?"

"Not really. Just the usual: my Saturday shopping trip, and then a visit to Mum on Sunday. Come to think of it, I have quite a boring life, don't I?"

"Oh, not at all! What about Brian? Won't you do something fun with him?"

Unfortunately, my lovely fiancé had been fairly absent for the last few weekends. "Probably not." I'd intended to sound casual but didn't quite manage it.

"He's still busy with some big project at work." He'd been working all hours recently and when he wasn't working, he was too exhausted to do anything.

"Oh, Marie, that's terrible." Anne came and perched on the opposite edge of my desk. It was her customary position when conversations got serious. I hadn't meant to make out that things were so bad they warranted an edge of the desk chat.

"No, it's fine!" I cheerfully waved a hand in front of my face and hoped she'd retreat. "Once this project is over, things will calm down." I forced a smile. Deep down I knew that once this project ended, another would begin. Brian worked in investment banking and his job was high-pressured and demanding. He was currently knee-deep in some big acquisition and it was eating its way into his social life and our relationship.

"You should talk to him, or things will only get worse. You don't want to marry a workaholic. Get him to cut back. He should at least have weekends free to spend time with you."

"He does usually, it's just the last few weeks that have been hectic. It'll be fine."

"They'll write that on your gravestone. *It'll be fine.* Sometimes you need to address your problems head on instead of waiting to see what happens." Anne was always spouting little gems of wisdom like this. It was like having my own personal agony aunt.

"Thanks for the advice. I will definitely think about it. Now come on, isn't it time to flip the sign to *open*? We'll have a queue out there if we're not careful." Anne chuckled as she moved towards the door. We both knew that we wouldn't have any customers for a while. The first hour was always slow. It would be phone calls and admin work for the next hour or two.

I thought about Anne's words as I looked through my emails. She was always full of unwanted advice but she'd got me thinking this time. Maybe I should talk to Brian. His workload had been steadily increasing and it was frustrating never to have his full attention. The trouble was he seemed stressed enough without me nagging him.

"Are you excited about Grace's visit?" Anne said, interrupting my thoughts.

"Yeah, I think so." My best friend Grace was flying in from New York to start planning her wedding, which would take place the following spring. I'd taken some time off work and told her I'd help out. I wasn't really sure what that would entail. Theoretically, I should be busy planning my own wedding. Brian and I had decided to get married abroad but we were struggling to choose the destination so there wasn't much planning going on.

"You don't sound too sure! Are you worried you'll miss me?"

"Ha! That has been playing on my mind! Actually, I get the feeling I'll be busier than I ever am at work. Just don't tell Greg." I paused as I thought about Grace. I should have been excited to see her, but her upcoming visit was making me nervous more than anything else. "It's never very relaxed with Grace these days." I chewed the end of my pen. "I feel like I'm constantly making excuses for myself and my life."

"Oh, but she's your best friend. I'm sure you'll have a lovely time. It'll be nice to have a proper catch up."

"You're probably right." I hoped I was overthinking things. Grace had been my best friend since primary school and she'd just always been in my life. I sometimes wondered, though, if we met now, whether we'd be friends at all.

I decided I ought to be productive and dragged my thoughts back to work. I spent an hour replying to emails before our first customers of the day arrived. As usually happened, the day got steadily busier and the time flew by. Before I knew it, I glanced at the door to see Jason arriving. I grabbed at the phone on my desk and pretended to be deep in conversation.

"Sorry, Jason." I screwed up my face as I moved the phone to my shoulder. "I'm in the middle of something here. I think it's going to take a while. Shall we postpone?"

"Really?" He stared at me with a hand on his hip. "We're still going through this little charade every time?"

I tried to look indignant before I gave up and replaced the phone on the desk. My acting skills clearly needed some work.

With a sigh, I went to change into my jogging gear.

Chapter 2

"How was your day?" I asked Jason as we ran down the main shopping street, dodging pedestrians as we went. My running skills had definitely improved. When I'd first started with Jason, I couldn't talk while jogging. My lungs didn't allow it.

"Oh, I've got this new client, Miss Whippy. She's a total nightmare."

"Miss Whippy?" I asked. "Like the ice cream?"

"Yeah. If you saw her hair, you'd understand. She's trying to get in shape for her wedding, like you."

"Good one, Jason!" We both knew that I was not trying to get in shape for my wedding. In fact I had no real desire to get in shape at all. I'd made peace with my size twelve figure a long time ago. I was no supermodel, but I'd never seen the point in obsessing over a bit of extra weight. After being bullied into working out with Jason, I'd gradually come around to the idea of a bit of exercise in my life. I felt healthier for it and I enjoyed the chats with Jason. Although, recently he spent a lot of time teasing me about my inability to choose a wedding destination.

"Come on, Marie, I'm dying to get myself a new hat!"

"Who said you're invited?" I laughed at him. I

wasn't entirely sure the hat comment was a joke either, what with Jason's odd dress sense. I'd never seen him 'off duty', so I couldn't really imagine him without sports clothes on, but he definitely prided himself on his unique and fairly effeminate style.

"How are the driving lessons going?" he asked, changing the subject. I registered the cheeky grin on his face.

"Anne told you, didn't she?"

"Told me what?" he asked with a look of mock-innocence.

"I don't need to drive anyway. I've already told Brian. I've managed this far without that particular ability. Why start now? It was all his bright idea in the first place."

"Come on," he said. "Tell me the story."

"How do I know that you don't have a nickname for me and tell your other clients entertaining stories about my life?"

"Oh, I definitely have a nickname for you! And yours are the best stories. Don't let me down now."

"Fine," I said. "So the driving instructor claims he has some sort of 'three strikes and you're out' rule, but I actually think that him giving me the boot is more a reflection on his teaching skills than my driving abilities."

"So you really did get dumped by your driving instructor? I didn't know if Anne was having fun with me."

"Clearly Brian found me the worst driving instructor in town."

"Clearly! So what were your three mistakes? Something about a lamppost, was it?"

"Reversed into it," I confessed. "Then there was an incident with the wing mirror … apparently they're more effective when they're attached to the car. I also scratched the door a bit on a tree."

"You drove into a lamppost *and* a tree?" He spluttered out a laugh.

"No, I didn't drive into a tree. I just parked badly and opened the door a bit too fiercely. He overreacted on that occasion."

"And the dog?" He didn't look at me as he asked.

"I knew I shouldn't have told Anne about that. I only told her because I was slightly traumatised. But the dog was fine. Hardly a scratch on him and I think he learned a valuable lesson about road safety."

"Stay off the road when Marie's behind the wheel?"

"Shut up! The dog really was fine. I only nudged him. In fact, I think technically he ran into the car. People overreacted again."

"I believe you! Anyway, that's four things, not three."

"Yeah but when the wing mirror happened he told me to pull over and was muttering about how he definitely couldn't teach me anymore, so I got a bit angry and opened the door pretty wildly into the tree …"

"Wow! Two scrapes in one lesson? I guess you're not his favourite person." He snorted with laughter. "Come on, let's put in a bit more effort for the home stretch, shall we?"

"No, I'm okay thanks." He'd already sprinted away from me. My fitness level really had improved a lot since I'd started training with Jason. The first few weeks were torturous. There was even a day I jogged right on to a bus just to get away from him. I don't really know what had come over me but I was gasping for breath and being shouted at by Jason, so when the bus pulled up at the stop, I dropped back and got on it.

Given how much I hate buses it felt like an 'out of the frying pan, into the fire' situation, but at the time I would've done anything to get away from Jason. I'd felt his eyes on me as the bus drove past him. It wasn't even going in the right direction. I got off a couple of stops later, when I felt like I'd put enough distance between me and my sadistic personal trainer. I'd wandered slowly home, feeling slightly guilty, but confident I would never have to see Jason again.

Unfortunately, he wasn't so easily deterred. Eventually, I resigned myself to having exercise – and Jason – in my life.

Jason was jogging up and down the front steps when I caught up to him.

"I'd invite you in," I said, "but …"

"It's fat club night. I know. And sadly I don't qualify to join." He gave me a cheeky grin as he lifted his T-shirt to flash his six-pack. "See you soon," he called over his shoulder as he jogged away, leaving me smiling after him.

End of sample.

Printed in Great
Britain
by Amazon

31604778R00123